More Critical Praise for Preston L. Allen

for *Jesus Boy*

"Heartfelt and occasionally hilarious, *Jesus Boy* is a tender masterpiece."
—Dennis Lehane, author of *Small Mercies*

"Generations of illicit sex run through this clever and wide-ranging book in which the flesh always triumphs . . . Surely no one does church sexy like Allen . . . Allen's writing by turns is solemn and funny . . . It would be easy for *Jesus Boy* to become fluffy satire but Allen keeps his characters real."
—*New York Times Book Review*

"Allen has created a consummate tragicomedy of African American family secrets and sorrows, and of faith under duress and wide open to interpretation. Perfect timing and crackling dialogue, as well as heartrending pain balanced by uproarious predicaments, make for a shout-hallelujah tale of transgression and grace, a gospel of lusty and everlasting love." —*Booklist*

"*Jesus Boy* is one of those books that makes you sit up and go . . . WHAT? No novel should be this enthralling. With a mesmerizing style, Preston L. Allen offers sentences that you reread because of their sheer enchantment and sense of wonder they invoke . . . in magical prose that lights up the pages. This is a novel unlike any I've ever read and among the very best of the decade. What a joy to read a book you can truly call a contemporary classic."
—Ken Bruen, author of *The Guards*

"Ten More Titles to Read Now: Think African American *Romeo and Juliet*, as played out in a devout Christian community."
—*O, The Oprah Magazine*

"This latest from Allen is hilarious . . . Scenes of preaching and singing in the church convey the boisterous fervor of African American gospel music and religious practice in a soulful, vibrant style . . . This is a very enjoyable and well-done novel; highly recommended." —*Library Journal*

"A riveting story of star-crossed love, *Jesus Boy* plumbs the hypocrisies and impossible stringencies of evangelical America with humor and no small amount of pathos. This novel is definitely a guilty pleasure."
—Cristina García, author of *Dreaming in Cuban*

for *Every Boy Should Have a Man*

"Allen . . . throws caution to the wind with his bizarre but exquisitely composed fable that uses transhumanism as the prism to reflect on the nature of humanity . . . Much like Pierre Boulle's 1963 novel *Planet of the Apes,* this novel is a sardonic parable on the nature and destiny of the species. A nimble fable whose bold narrative experiment is elevated by its near-biblical language and affectionate embrace of our inherent flaws." —*Kirkus Reviews*

"Imaginative, versatile, and daring, Allen raids the realms of myth and fairy tales in this topsy-turvy speculative fable . . . With canny improvisations on 'Jack and the Beanstalk,' 'The Epic of Gilgamesh,' and *Alice in Wonderland,* Allen sharpens our perceptions of class divides, racism, enslavement, and abrupt and devastating climate change to create a delectably adventurous, wily, funny, and wise cautionary parable."   —*Booklist*

"Allen's concise book's power lies within its understated irony, never more heavy-handed than a preacher's admonition that 'a world without mans is a world without us all.' The plain narrative and relationship between boy and female man, rounded out with humor and occasional (sometimes literal) bite, promises to be a sleeper favorite among speculative audiences."
—*Publishers Weekly*

"An imaginative and honest epic, weaving together biblical stories, fantasy, poetry, and fairy tales with a touch of realism . . . Allen asks us to question the assumptions, -isms, and contradictions of the modern world . . . Recalling the humanitarian concerns of Octavia Butler's *Fledgling* and the poetry of Ovid's *Metamorphosis,* this book will appeal to readers of literary fiction and fantasy."   —*Library Journal*

"Allen has crafted a highly imaginative, unsettling work of social satire that . . . utilizes a speculative fable as a way to muse on race, slavery, civil rights, and even climate change . . . *Every Boy Should Have a Man* is James Baldwin meets Aldous Huxley, a twisted contortion of a weird fairy-tale future gone wrong, all told from high atop the mountain in a sort of New Testament prose. As the mixologist of this mad and unpredictable genre tableau, Allen has navigated into wholly uncharted territory. He comments on everything from slave ownership to pet ownership to the way we treat our planet and ourselves. His novel is ambitious yet understated, cautionary while rarely politically preachy. *Every Boy Should Have a Man* is that rare novel that is derived from such a disparate scope of literary influences that it waxes entirely original."   —*Chicago Tribune*

for *All or Nothing*

"As with Frederick and Steven Barthelme's disarming gambling memoir, *Double Down*, the chief virtue of *All or Nothing* is its facility in enlightening nonbelievers, showing how this addiction follows recognizable patterns of rush and crash, but with a twist—the buzz is in the process, not the result ... As a cartographer of autodegradation, Allen takes his place on a continuum that begins, perhaps, with Dostoyevsky's *Gambler*, courses through Malcolm Lowry's *Under the Volcano*, William S. Burroughs's *Junky*, the collected works of Charles Bukowski and Hubert Selby Jr., and persists in countless novels and (occasionally fabricated) memoirs of our puritanical, therapized present. Like Dostoyevsky, Allen colorfully evokes the gambling milieu—the chained (mis)fortunes of the players, their vanities and grotesqueries, their quasi-philosophical ruminations on chance. Like Burroughs, he is a dispassionate chronicler of the addict's daily ritual, neither glorifying nor vilifying the matter at hand."   —*New York Times Book Review*

"Dark and insightful ... The well-written novel takes the reader on a chaotic ride as ... Allen reveals how addiction annihilates its victims and shows that winning isn't always so different from losing."   —*Publishers Weekly*

"A gambler's hands and heart perpetually tremble in this raw story of addiction. 'We gamble to gamble. We play to play. We don't play to win.' Right there, P, desperado narrator of this crash-'n'-burn novel, sums up the madness ... Allen's brilliant at conveying the hothouse atmosphere of hell-bent gaming. Fun time in the Inferno."   —*Kirkus Reviews*

"Allen has done for gambling what William S. Burroughs did for narcotic addiction. He's gotten into the heart of the darkness and shown us what it feels like to be trapped, to be haunted, to live without choice. Allen is relentless and unsparing in his depiction of the life of a gambling addict, from the magical thinking to the visceral thrill of risking it all. And now the world will know what we in Miami have known for a long time: Preston L. Allen is so good a writer it's scary."

—John Dufresne, author of *Johnny Too Bad*

"By turns harrowing, illuminating, and endearing, Preston L. Allen's *All or Nothing* is more than a gut punch, it's a damn good book."

—Maggie Estep, author of *Alice Fantastic*

I DISAPPEARED THEM

BY PRESTON L. ALLEN

BROOKLYN, NEW YORK

This is a work of fiction. All names, characters, places, and incidents are the product of the author's imagination. Any resemblance to real events or persons, living or dead, is entirely coincidental.

Published by Akashic Books
©2024 Preston L. Allen
All rights reserved

ISBN: 978-1-63614-161-9
Library of Congress Control Number: 2023946523
First printing

Akashic Books
Brooklyn, New York
Instagram, Twitter, Facebook: AkashicBooks
info@akashicbooks.com
www.akashicbooks.com

To Dawn,
my first reader, my final proofreader,
my life partner, my love

I kill whores mostly,
and friends who sleep with my wife.
—Edgar L. Jackson

THE HUNTER

Eduardo

July 5, 2001

The dead man is Eduardo, and he drives an American car. It is a Ford, a roomy car, though Eduardo is not tall, standing exactly 5'7" from toe to head. He weighs 198 pounds, which is heavy for his height. In his charcoal-gray bespoke suit, you cannot tell, but Eduardo the bank officer is obese according to the charts.

Seconds after Eduardo exits his car, the hunter emerges from the alley.

—Eduardo lives in an apartment building on Aragon Avenue in Brickell just south of downtown Miami. In the 1920s, the apartment building was the mansion of a millionaire who made his money in steel. The lobby they enter was once a ballroom. It boasted polished black-and-white-tiled floors, a magnificent curved staircase, and a resplendent crystal chandelier that still hangs from its high cathedral ceiling. Eighty years later, there are still no security cameras in the lobby of the converted mansion.

Suddenly Eduardo turns. The hunter looks down, looks up, looks away, adjusts his cap. Eduardo walks on.

—Slow and joyless are the footfalls of Eduardo. For him, it is the end of a tedious workday. He is in familiar surroundings, and his mind is elsewhere. His mind is on his troubles with his ex who seems happier without him. Why should he care?

She's his ex. It should not matter that she is better off without him, but it does.

Last night Eduardo appeared in the hunter's dream. Eduardo had no hands or feet in the hunter's dream.

—The hunter follows Eduardo into a fancy jazz age elevator framed in bronze leaf frills. Eduardo carries a briefcase, his favorite. It is the last gift she gave him before she left. The hunter is a pizza man. He carries a pizza-warmer bag on one shoulder, his left. He wears a black T-shirt and matching cap, cheap, no-name-brand jeans, and surgical gloves. Eduardo nods at the hunter, noting the cheap jeans, missing the surgical gloves. The hunter nods back, his face a blank. They get off on the second floor and Eduardo opens his door with a key.

The hunter drops the warmer bag and shoves him inside.

—There is a snarl and a flash of white teeth.

The hunter grabs Eduardo and holds him around the neck. There is a noiseless flailing of arms by Eduardo as he fights back. The cap is knocked from the hunter's head. He gets a hand in the eye and for a moment sees stars. Eduardo clutches desperately at the hunter's hands around his neck.

"Get off me! Help—!"

The hunter slaps a hand over Eduardo's mouth and sinks the needle in his neck. A little blood spurts. He notes where it falls. Later, he'll have to clean that up.

Eduardo collapses. His head has become groggy, his voice weak. "Is it about Jenny?" he says.

The hunter does not answer. He picks up his warmer bag and matching cap, and shuts the door for privacy.

—Though Eduardo has been divorced for a year and three

days, the apartment still has the woman's touch. The peaches-and-cream couch that still carries her smell. The matching wall art she chose. The framed photographs of her beautiful face that Eduardo found too precious to part with. The angelic smile. The eyes, green and gemlike. He was with her yesterday at the Fourth of July barbecue, though he was told to stay away. She looked even more beautiful in real life.

The hunter knows how it is. The hunter has been there.

He understands love's great power to hold, a hold so strong that you'd humiliate yourself by going to her family's backyard party on the Fourth of July. You would endure the subtle rebukes of her mother, the giggling insinuations of her teen sister, the threatening looks from her father. You would shake her new lover's hand, pat him on the back. Smile. Say nice things about the weather, which is cool for July because of the rain. Oh, but yesterday it was a hot one.

They find your fawning transparent, your presence offensive. The stern father tells you to leave or you'll get a beating you won't forget. In the car on the way home you shed tears knowing they still hate you, but it was worth it. Anything to be near her again. You love her, Eduardo. Always have. Always will. That's why you put her in the hospital half a dozen times before she finally got fed up and left you.

Beneath the green of her gemlike eyes, there is red from the strain of living with you.

She lost the baby.

The hunter will not punish you for that crime, Eduardo. That crime is between a husband and a wife. The divorce has already punished you for that crime.

The hunter has come bearing gifts. In the van, there is a mattress to lay you on, straps to bind you with, and tools to hack your limbs and separate them from your body with. And flowers.

Periwinkles.

"Is it about Jenny?" Eduardo says again when the hunter comes back to him. His breathing is shallow. The hallucinations have set in. Jenny stands next to the pizza man, holding his hand, smiling. Without warning, Jenny turns into a green-eyed balloon and floats away, still smiling. "Is it about money?"

The hunter does not answer.

He watches for two and a half minutes until Eduardo's eyelids close. Then he stands him gently, like supporting a friend who has drunk too much at a party, leans him on his shoulder, and walks him out of the apartment.

They exit the building through the service door at the rear and enter the alley where the van awaits. The sun lingers low in the summer sky. The shadows in the alley stretch long, shading the face of a staggering Eduardo. He tries to speak, but he can't fight the drug. When he passes out, he becomes suddenly heavy on the hunter's shoulder and almost hits the ground.

The hunter hefts Eduardo into the van, flops him onto the mattress in the back, stuffs the towel in his mouth, and binds his hands together with the leather straps.

—Back at the restaurant, he parks across the street and watches the other drivers enter and exit their cars, going on deliveries, returning from deliveries.

There is a moment of indecision. Will he be able to go through with it? Well, it must be done.

In the back of the van where it is cool and dark, Eduardo stirs, blinking back to consciousness. There is a towel stuffed in his mouth. His arms and legs strain against leather straps. Who did this?

He lifts his face to the black T-shirt, the matching cap, and he remembers. The pizza man did this.

That baffled but comical look on Eduardo's face, the look of someone at a surprise birthday party about to laugh when the lights are switched on—that look vanishes when he spies the pizza man's handsaw and the set of polished and well-sharpened knives.

The hunter selects the carving knife.

The towel muffles the dead man's scream.

When it is all over, he gives the dead man his flowers.

Periwinkles.

"Just like this," the hunter says. "Bob is gonna get it just like this."

—The hunter arrives home to his small apartment, and his wife, who holds the phone to her ear, sees him and sets it in its cradle.

"Who?" the hunter says.

"No one special," his wife says.

He knows she's lying. At best it's one of her trash sisters. At worst it's Bob. It's probably Bob. He says, "Is Junior in bed?"

"Is it one of those nights?"

"It's one of those nights."

His nervous shakes are gone, and his hands are steady again. When he reaches for her, she pats her distended stomach.

"Remember, I'm eight months pregnant."

"I'll be careful."

"Don't be careful," his wife says. "Be good."

While their natures are separate and apart on most things, on this they agree: love, for a moment, makes the pain go away. In spite of all that's happened, they do love each other. An injury to pride, however, is not easily healed. The hunter lifts his wife from the settee and heads in the direction of their bedroom.

There are only two rooms in the small apartment, plus the living room and a small kitchen that doubles as a laundry room because of the rickety washing machine next to the ancient stove. He kisses his wife on the mouth and tickles her as they enter their bedroom. She tries not to laugh, but she does.

They are good in their bedroom, though not so good it would wake Junior.

Afterward, he asks her to marry him. Once again, his wife says no.

The washing machine makes the rickety sound as it spins.

And except for the murder of Eduardo Gomez, who is the hunter's first kill, it is a normal day.

The Baby

"The baby's name when it is born," says the hunter, "shall be Zander."

"Zoe," says his wife, "if it's a girl. Or maybe Bobbi Sue."

"You're kidding, right? Don't kid around like that."

She closes her mouth and turns away from him on the bed.

"You should be careful what you say," he says.

And well she should because Bob is gonna get it. His wife, if she's not careful, might get it too.

The Call

It is two days later. It is 10:00 p.m.

Raindrops pummel the top of the black van as it approaches the phone booth outside a porn shop on 163rd Street in North Miami. The hunter steps out and a curtain of rain closes over his eyes. In the phone booth, he makes a call to the Miami-Dade PD.

"I killed a man."

"Who? What?" the officer says.

"Be silent and listen," the hunter says in an artificial voice, a kind of farcical snarl. "He was a wife beater. He won't be missed."

The officer is silent and the hunter proceeds to tell them where in the Everglades the dead man can be found.

"And who are you?" the officer says. "What should we call you?"

Lightning from the torrent brightens the night sky and thunder rolls.

"Call me Periwinkle," the hunter says.

The Note

He calls his favorite reporter at the *Herald*, but gets a recorded message.

"I'm away from my desk right now. Please leave a message at the sound of the tone."

"I just wanted to talk, but I guess you're away from your desk. I'm a tormented soul. I'm in pain."

—That night in his notes, he writes, *And so it begins.*

And so it does, although it began years ago.

The Slap

There was a girl.

Back in eighth grade before the hunter was a hunter, he had a friend Gerardo, whom he called Bryce . . .

Bryce, we'll say.

They had been friends since childhood. By eighth grade Gerardo had become handsome and the hunter had remained the same. It was summer in Palmetto Cove, a medium-sized, mixed-race, working-class South Florida city, and the middle school took the honors students on their annual trip to the famous amusement park up in Tampa.

And Gerardo had a girlfriend and the hunter had *Bryce.*

—Oh, it was to be a great day of fun and rides, but Bryce wanted to spend the day with his girl, who had a friend for the hunter, how nice.

So Bryce walked with his girl, always the prettier girl, and the hunter walked with the friend of Bryce's girl.

The hunter and the friend were behind Bryce and his girl most of the day, blushing witnesses to their cop-feels and kisses. This girl who was the friend of Bryce's girl, she was gawky and a head or so taller than the hunter, and he found her to be quite unattractive compared to Bryce's girl, but she sat a few desks away from him in math and had borrowed a number 2 lead pencil from him once, so he agreed to the arrangement.

As the day of fun progressed, they grew less uncomfortable with each other. Their conversations, though strained at first, had become pleasant as they watched the smooching of Bryce and his girl and at times made jokes about it.

When it was time for lunch, Bryce and his girl snuck off somewhere to kiss, and the hunter and the less pretty girl sat down across from each other at a stone table with colored marble tiles for a top. He offered her a nibble of his PB and J because she hadn't brought lunch. She had come with money, however. At the food stand she bought a hamburger, an ice-cold drink in a jumbo cup, and a Kit Kat bar, which she broke in half and held out to him.

"Here, take it."

It was high noon and hot, the Kit Kat bar was already melting, but he took it and put it in his mouth. The mild chocolate swirled around his tongue and the thin wafer crunched between his teeth. It was the best candy bar he'd ever had.

He thought they had made a connection, though he had to admit he had no experience in that area at all, so he might've been wrong. They were standing closer to each other now. They were laughing into each other's faces now. He was finding her boyish-cut brown hair, dull brown eyes, and inappropriately cute nose a less unappealing composition by the minute. He presumed she was finding admirable qualities in his rather unremarkable features as well—a dog lick of stringy black hair sitting above a pale face peppered with freckles.

When the sun went down, they found themselves seated side by side on the Sunshine State Spinner, the centerpiece of the amusement park. It had enormous, hard-plastic carriages shaped like hemispheres of citrus fruit that lifted them and dipped them and spun them, and they whirled.

He gripped the safety bar. "Ahh woooo!"

She gripped his hand. "Ahh woooo!"

They leaned into each other, their shoulders touching. They cried, "Ahh woooo!"

As the hunter and his Kit Kat girl spun in their plastic kumquat, just ahead of them in their own whirling tangerine, Bryce and his girl smooched deliciously. The idea that was growing in the hunter's mind was one of imitation and experimentation. He would attempt to kiss her.

She did seem to like him, and her friend was smooching just ahead with his friend, and though she was not the most attractive girl, his gaze traced the sunburned skin around her eyes down to that embarrassingly cute nose, down to her mouth where the sunburned flesh became pouty pink lips. As her hand clutched his in the excitement of the moment, he glimpsed something appealing beneath the rough exterior. The Kit Kat girl was just like him, overshadowed by a more attractive best friend.

In the gift shop, he had purchased for her a teddy bear on a string. It was silly, but she had picked it up and made a funny joke about it before setting it back on the shelf with the other silly, colorful things. "This is just so cute," she had said. On the sneak, he slipped the cashier his last five dollars and quickly stuffed the silly thing in his pocket. He would give it to her in this whirling, hard-plastic kumquat and they would kiss.

It was nighttime and colored lights were blinking all around them. The rock music blared. The wind howled against their faces. He reached into his pocket and gripped the silly bear on a string in his hand. He raised his arm and the Kit Kat girl slapped his face.

Whap!

—After their plastic fruit ceased its spinning and the ride was over, the Kit Kat girl stumbled in her haste to her friend,

Bryce's girl, and, gesturing crazily, whispered into the pretty girl's ear words that were no doubt scathing.

When she glanced back at him, the hunter was hopeful, but she raised her middle finger and mouthed, *Ass clown.*

Bryce in amazement asked him: "What did you do to her? You didn't try to touch her you-know-whats, did you?"

"I did nothing to her." The hunter's head was still groggy from the dizzying ride, the bafflement. His face still stung from the slap, the embarrassment. "I did not touch her you-know-whats."

He opened his hand, revealing the silly teddy bear on a string. Bryce took it from him. "I'll fix it."

"You'll make it worse."

He had only wanted a kiss. He had only wanted to be normal like Bryce, who always got the pretty girl.

He watched as Bryce walked to where the girls stood talking to each other, near the booth where tickets to ride the Sunshine Choo-Choo Express were sold. A noisy queue of children with pinwheel hats of green and orange snaked around them to get to the ticket seller, a dark-brown woman in clown makeup, overalls, and a candy-striped conductor's cap who cried, "Get your tickets! Get your tickets! Now boarding the Sunshine Choo-Choo Express!"

The slapper's back was to the hunter again. The pretty girl, who was thinner and taller, watched him over her friend's shoulder. Her bronze hair was worn upswept and held in place with a black-and-white spiral hair tie. Feathered bangs fluttered above her smiling blue-gray eyes. She waved at him with her fingers.

The hunter blushed and quickly turned away from the face of his future wife.

"Get your tickets! Get your tickets!"

2002

David

At the entrance of the small, family-owned hardware store, the hunter is met by a hand-painted sign: *Beware! Protect your glasses!*

Yes. The jack-move twins. He's heard of them.

Two boys from the mean streets of Hialeah. Hialeah street urchins, no more than twelve or thirteen, terrorizing department stores. One is brown. The other can pass for white. They're not twins at all. Best friends is all.

What they do is, they snatch chains from people wearing glasses. The one who is almost white snatches the chain from your neck and makes a dash for the exit. Before you can give chase, the brown one snatches the glasses from your face and hurls them across the room. Now your vision is gone as well as your chain. How are you going to give chase? *Who* are you going to chase? You don't even know what they look like.

Bueno bye to your chain, as they say in Hialeah.

Of late their criminal endeavors have grown particularly spiteful. The jack-move twins have begun crushing the glasses or hawking up a good one and spitting it on them.

To combat the prolific pair of snatch-and-dash bandits, the stores have beefed up security, installed cameras if they didn't already have them, and posted warnings like the hand-painted sign at the entrance of the Handyman Ricky Hardware Store on 49th Street in Hialeah.

Beware! Protect your glasses!

"Just punks," the hunter mutters as he enters the hardware store. "I wish they would try that with me."

He heads to the yard tools aisle though he's not looking for a shovel or a rake. The yard tools aisle is where they keep the hatchets. The handsaw warps too easily, he has found. He needs an upgrade to a better tool. He overhears two men carrying on a conversation in house paints, which is the next aisle over.

One says, "Now they're using mace."

The other one says, "Mace?"

"The guy wasn't wearing glasses, so they used mace."

"Jheeze. That's horrible."

"I'm telling you."

"These kids. These kids. It drives me crazy."

"Kids have no discipline today. The parents aren't around. They're raising themselves. That's why it happens. Cops need to do something."

"Cops? Don't blame it on us. Our hands are tied. We clean up. We file reports."

The hunter speaks through the shelf of hatchets to the aisle of paint, interrupting them: "And what good is that? By the time cops get there, the crime has already been committed."

One of the men pushes aside a can of cardinal red, and a thick face with narrow features appears. "You're right, friend."

The unseen one says, "Wadd'ya think we should do?"

"You've got to stand tall."

"Yes, stand tall."

"Gird up your loins."

"*Gird?* What's that?"

"Look them in the eye and say—"

Thick Face says, "And say just what exactly, friend?"

The unseen one says, "Plus, you can't look 'em in the eye. Yer glasses are gone, or you got mace in yer eye."

Before the hunter can answer, they push the can of cardinal red back in place and resume talking to each other.

The hunter does not take a brush-off lightly, and he knows that he has been brushed off, but he doesn't really have an answer. All he knows is that he doesn't wear glasses. He does, however, wear a chain, the gold chain his dada gave him. They had better not try that mace stunt with him.

The hunter grips a hatchet and balances it in both hands. He exchanges it for another and balances that one for comparison. They are both good tools for the price. On the other hand, the first has a heavier, narrower head. Better for precise cutting. He chooses the first one and carries it to the register.

—At Winn-Dixie on the way home, he picks up a box of Corn Flakes and a pack of peppermint gum for himself, a box of Cocoa Puffs for Junior, a tin of Taster's Choice for his wife, and a pack of Pampers pull-ups for Zoe Yasmine who has taken her first steps.

The mop, bleach, Lysol, and air freshener are for later.

They are arguing more than usual. She is pregnant again. This one will make three kids. No more after this, she insists. No more.

He insists there will be more. He loves kids. Good night hugs, apple juice, and shitty diapers—all of it. Children are precious.

"The apartment is too small," she says.

"We'll move. We'll get a bigger place," he says.

"We can't afford to move. We can't afford a bigger place. You're just a pizza man."

"Watch what you say."

"Can't you see I'm not happy?" she says. "I have other options, you know."

"Other options?" he says. "Like Bob?"

"What about Bob? That's over, I told you. You're crazy. Get out of my house! Get out!"

He drives to the pizzeria, the phrase *other options* playing in his head like discordant wind chimes. When he gets there, he pulls on his black T-shirt and dons the matching cap. He inspects himself in the mirror. He adjusts his cap. He looks snazzy.

His last delivery is at midnight, but there is a delivery he must make after that, so he keeps the panel van. He's going to do it right this time.

He's going to bag it, then pack it.

—He arrives at David's at 12:31.

David lives in a neighborhood where the trees are leafy and the bushes are overgrown. On the street behind David's there is an empty lot. Another palatial home is going up. The hunter parks his van in the shadows, gets out, and slips onto David's property through the connecting hedges in the backyard, where he waits.

David is already at home, the hunter can tell from the dimmed lights and the swaying silhouettes. David is having an affair with a married woman, and she is here again tonight.

The married woman, who stands a head or so taller than David, was here the night six months ago when the hunter delivered the pizza. She had reddish hair and was leggy and skinny. The large breasts spilling from her lacy top were a gift from her lover David, who is a plastic surgeon.

"Your ad says pizza's free if it's late," David had said. He was maybe 5'7", thick around the waist, tan-faced, and balding. The three crumpled tens clutched in his hand were just enough to pay for the pizza without a tip. "It's a minute late."

"It took two minutes for you to open the door."

"I was otherwise occupied." David winked at the hunter and reached back and smacked the skinny woman's butt.

"Ouch," she said, twisting with giggles.

"That's no excuse to keep a pizza man waiting." The hunter swung the warmer bag resting on his left shoulder down to his midriff and balanced it on his hip. In one expert move, he unzipped the bag and pulled out the cardboard pizza box—a gesture like pulling something from the crotch of his trousers. "Here's your pizza."

The box balanced there, warm and erect on the hunter's hip, the delicious smell of Italian spices, anchovies, and melted cheese wafting out from it. No one touched it.

David's mistress, sensing something dangerous about this pizza man, had tightened the loose lingerie around her thick chest and gone back inside.

"What if I don't pay you, wise guy?" David shoved the dollar bills into a pocket of his silk housecoat, which was black with a Japanese dragon on the front. "What if I just take the pizza and close the door?" he said.

"Company policy says I can't do anything about it, Dr. Perez."

"How did you know I'm a doctor?" David said.

"It says so on that certificate behind you on the wall."

On the wall behind David was his surgeon's certificate, framed in gold, but he lived in a large house.

"How did you . . . ?" David began.

The wall was too far away to see, and the lights were dimmed for an evening of romance. This guy might've had a woman in his life who needed her nose chiseled or her breasts enlarged, and that's where he knew him from. Or maybe this guy—and here is the part that troubled David—maybe this guy, this pizza man, had been *inside* the house.

But how? The house had an alarm system, right?

"Wait here," David said, cautiously lifting the warm box from the hunter's hip.

The hunter's eyes were hard and cold, and so filled with hate that David turned away.

David took the pizza inside and returned a minute later waving enough dollar bills for a large tip. The hunter looked down at the money. He took it with a grunt that might have been *Thanks* and walked back to the black van. As David watched the hunter drive away, he made up his mind.

That week, David got a guard dog.

—Tonight the hunter waits for the red-haired woman to leave and for David to fall asleep.

At 2:15, the hunter emerges from the shadows of the backyard. The new guard dog, Lobo, was drugged earlier and sleeps quietly in his doghouse. The neighborhood is dark but safe, and stingy David purchased the cheapest kind of alarm system, one tied to the phone line with the box outside. As he did six months ago, the hunter disables the phone line, pries open a window, and climbs inside.

At 2:17, David looks up in horror as the new hatchet with the heavier, narrower head descends. "You're the pizza man!"

"And you're the whoremonger." The hatchet lands, missing the heart, but chops a lung, severing the arteries. David drowns in his own blood. *Fast and efficient,* Dada says. *Like killing a deer.*

By 2:35, ten or so pints of blood have been collected in mason jars and tidily arranged in a cardboard box, though some remains on the sheets and the carpet. Later, he'll have to clean that up.

By 3:15, the house has been cleaned and made tidy. Everything is wiped down with Lysol. Everything is lemony fresh.

By 3:17, the periwinkles have been stuffed in the dead man's pockets, his body parts bagged and packed in the van.

Bag it, then pack it.

By 3:18, the telephone line has been reconnected as it was six months ago when he did the test run, and the job is done.

—When he returns home, he sticks the key in the door, but the chain is on. He pushes against the door, rattling the chain. Angry blue-gray eyes peer at him through the crack.

"Don't say it," she says.

She unhooks the chain, but blocks his entrance with her body. She is nearly as tall as he is. She used to be an athlete and has big feet and big hands. She wears her midnight-black hair in a pixie bob, but she is no pixie.

He says, "I'm assistant manager now. I've got responsibilities. I had to go to the warehouse."

"At four in the morning?"

"I had to go to—"

"Don't even say it." She puts her hands on his chest and pushes him back when he moves to embrace her. "See? See? This is why I'll never marry you. You're broke. You have no ambition. And all of this sneaking around. All of this lying."

—In the morning it is Sunday, and she has no schoolchildren to sing to, no private students to teach, no classes at the community college to go to. Today she is all his.

"You come home at all hours. All of this lying and asking about Bob. Who were *you* with?" she says. "Broke. Unambitious. Weak."

"Watch your mouth."

"Or what?"

By noon, he can't take it anymore.

He runs out of the apartment like it's on fire and slams the door. She jerks it open and leans her head out. "Too afraid to talk, huh? That's right. Get out. You'd better leave. When you come back, I may not be here. Bob is a real man, and you know it. *Asshole!*"

He ends up outside M. Jolene's, a classy department store in the high-end section of the mall across the corridor from where the Asians sell gold and precious gems by the ounce. What it would be like to have money. What it would be like to treat his wife to fancy restaurants, to treat her to a spa so she can relax her long legs and get a back massage, to treat her to a chunk of this expensive jewelry the Asians sell by weight. Maybe she would treat him better. Maybe she would marry him. What it would be like to shop for her in places like M. Jolene's. What a fantasy. Most items in M. Jolene's would squeeze their tight budget, but the name *M. Jolene's*. The name might fix it.

Inside M. Jolene's, the tinny elevator music plays a song he is familiar with. He hums the tune, but he can't remember the name. It is a love song. Michael Jackson. Paul McCartney. "The Girl Is Mine."

The girl is his. That day in Tampa, Bryce had her, but now she's his. The prettiest girl is his. The doggone girl is his.

In the women's shoes aisle, the fuzzy bedroom slippers catch his eye. They are silver with bronze puffs. They are beautiful. They are priced at one dollar less than last night's tips. Her big feet will look good in them. These will fix it.

He picks up a pair in size 11, and a jack-move twin snatches Dada's chain from his neck.

Bueno bye, chain.

—He clutches at his neck for his dead father's chain. He

sees the other one aiming the mace. It's coming at him like
snot from someone else's sneeze. He turns away, but not fast
enough.

"Ow!"

It burns his face, blinding him, but adrenaline quickens
his reflexes. A grasp in the dark, and he's got the boy's hand.

"Oh you—!" The hunter's blind grasping finds the boy's
other hand. "You little punk."

The brown boy's hands are caught by the blinded hunter.
The boy kicks and spits and curses. "Lemme go!"

The hunter has the boy's hands, and he is strong. One
flinch, and he breaks all the fingers on both hands.

Bueno bye, fingers.

—He pulls the broken hands into himself until he feels the
boy's wrists, which he breaks, and then the forearms, which
he disjoints. His plan is to rip the boy's arms off, and then
do the legs. He will rip the legs off and fold them neatly into
a butcher's sack as he did to David's last night. Then he will
find the other jack-move twin, retrieve his dead father's chain,
rip him apart, and he gets the bag too. They can join David in
the muddy water of the Everglades. They can all wait there
for Bob. Bob's day is coming. Bob is gonna get it too.

Bueno bye, Bob.

—The security guards arrive and wrestle him off the broken
jack-move twin. In short order, an ambulance arrives, the police arrive.

"The Girl Is Mine" has ended. A new song plays. "You
Light Up My Life." The hunter knows this song, but he's in
no mood for humming. It is a song his wife sang in high
school when she was in chorus. It is a song she sometimes
still sings, but not to him.

The ambulance, its lights flashing red and white, hauls the broken jack-move twin away.

The other jack-move twin sits in the back of the police cruiser, his face red and snotty from crying. They found him in the parking lot, just a little boy, crying for his ripped-apart partner.

The hunter pounds on the window. "Where's my chain? Hey, you! Where's my chain?"

—"I want my chain. It was my father's," the hunter says to the EMT, a silent woman in green, as she dabs his face with a soft cloth soaked in a greasy solution that smells like spoiled milk but cools his skin, giving him some relief from the burning. "Oh, Dada. The chain," the hunter says again.

The police officer jotting down notes looks up. "It's you. Still girding, I see," he says to the hunter.

Squinting to focus, the hunter recognizes the thick face, the thin nose, and matches it to the voice he heard yesterday behind the can of cardinal-red paint. Thick Face is the cop jotting down notes. Thick Face is too late. Thick Face is here to clean up. Thick Face tells the hunter the thing he wants least to hear: "The little thug says he dropped the chain. He says he doesn't know where, but rest assured we'll find it."

The hunter shakes his head. "I can't accept that."

He could just kill them. They took Dada's chain. If he could just get Dada's chain back. He almost killed them, my God. He didn't want to hurt them. They are children, no different than he and Bryce when they were that age. Best friends. Best friends are precious, but Dada's chain. He could just kill them.

When his eyes clear, the hunter searches the parking lot for three hours while the M. Jolene's employees look on. They know that he searches in vain, but no one says this to him, for he is the man who broke human bones with his bare hands.

Finally, the store manager appears. His name tag says, *Hi I'm Fredrick.*

"We have a policy," Fredrick the store manager says. "At M. Jolene's, we guarantee the safety of our customers, and clearly we did not keep you or your property safe. How much would you say it was worth?" Fredrick is brown and his shoes are sneakers, the expensive kind that M. Jolene's sells. "I'm sure M. Jolene's can reimburse you at least two hundred and fifty dollars. Maybe three hundred. How about that? Or maybe we can replace the chain. We sell chains."

The hunter shoots Fredrick the store manager a deadly look. "I wouldn't care if you gave me a thousand dollars. I wouldn't care if you went across the hall and got me a chunk of that expensive stuff the Asians sell. I want *that* chain, Fredrick. I want my dada's chain. Can you do that?"

—At home, Zoe rests peacefully in her crib, and Junior plays with a toy fire truck on the floor. Tears leak from his eyes as they leak from his father's eyes.

The hunter's wife says, "Don't worry, they'll find it. You're a hero. Everybody's calling you a hero."

He says, "I don't feel like a hero."

"But you are." His wife wipes the tears from his burned face. She kisses him and means it this time. She hasn't mentioned their fight, where he was last night, that Bob is a real man, or *other options* all evening. She tenderly whispers, "I love my new slippers."

She also loves the three hundred dollars from M. Jolene's and has already decided they will spend it on a diaper service for the baby when it comes. She doesn't want to go through what she went through with the first two.

There are other bills, but the three hundred will go to the new diaper service if it makes her happy. He wants her to be happy. It hurts him that Bob made her happy. It hurts that she calls Bob a real man, but not him, the man who stands by her and their two children, one of whom is Bob's. He loves Zoe, but Zoe is Bob's kid.

Bob is not a real man just because he got you pregnant. A real man is a father to his children like Dada was to me.

The hunter rubs his wife's baby bump affectionately.

At least this one is mine.

And he continues to weep.

Weak Man

"Just a thought," he says later that evening. "That kid in lockup. Him in that cell with all those perverts. With the three hundred dollars we got from M. Jolene's, we could bail him out."

"Don't even think it," his wife says. She's on the phone with the twenty-four-hour diaper service. She covers the receiver with a hand. "Where do you get these crazy ideas? I'm putting my foot down."

The way she says this amuses him. Her feet are size 11, which is above average for a woman. She frowns as she finishes registering for diaper service. When she says, "Okay, thank you," into the phone, he reaches for her. She knocks his hand away.

"I'm angry with you. The way you waste money."

"They are twelve, thirteen—just children."

"Children who spray mace and snatch chains," she says, touching his face where it was burned. It is moist with sweat and tears. She sets the phone in its cradle and rolls over on her side with her back to him. "It was a nice thought, though."

They are separate and apart on most things, but on this they agree: love means never having to say you're a weak man.

His arm falls across her belly. His fingers massage her skin.

"The baby will be here in two months," she says.

"I'll be gentle," he says.

They say together, "Don't be gentle. Be good."
And they laugh.

Compulsions

It is two days later. It is 10:00 p.m.

The heat is on him like a burning blanket. He can't throw it off.

He removes his shirt and ties it around his waist. That helps a little. He enters the phone booth outside a convenience store on 79th Street. His fake voice wheezes like an asthmatic and cracks like ancient plaster: "I killed a man. A whoremonger."

"Wait. I've got some questions for you." The officer is female this time and she is brown, he can tell from the low, bluesy timbre of her voice, which awakens the fine hairs on his skin. "I want to know why you're doing this," she says.

"Be silent and listen, or this conversation is over."

The female officer becomes silent, and the hunter proceeds to tell her where in the Everglades Dr. David Perez can be found.

"Who are you?" she says afterward.

"Periwinkle," he says.

"So you're not going to tell us your real name."

"You can call me Periwinkle."

"Why are you doing this, Periwinkle?"

Lightning cracks and thunder rumbles in the distance.

"Adultery is still a crime on the books in Florida. It does incalculable damage to families."

"*Incalculable*," she says, testing the word, wondering at it.

"It hurts children," he says.

"No one gets arrested for it anymore. There are good people who have had affairs. There are good people who have made a mistake."

"A child molester is next."

"Oh, you avenge children?"

"Are there any child molesters who have made a mistake?" he says. "Should I not save a child?"

"That's *our* job," the brown voice says. "Periwinkle, tell us who the molester is and we'll pick him up." Her voice thrills him like the hunt. It thrills like the kill. He could listen to her brown voice all night, but the call is being traced. "Periwinkle, are you still there?"

He hangs up.

He opens his mouth and takes in the rain, which is falling gently now. The rain is hot, but it cools him, and he puts back on his shirt. In the van, his butt sloshes in the wet seat. He takes off his jeans and underwear and hangs them in the back. He dries off his butt and balls with a towel he keeps in the van. It is more comfortable now when he sits, though the seat is still wet.

There is a popping like gunshots. He freezes. It's only firecrackers left over from the Fourth of July. Then comes the sound of sirens. He slips a stick of peppermint gum in his mouth and steps on the gas.

—That night in his notes he writes, *She has a voice that I can listen to all night.*

He puts his notes away, turns off the light, and yawning, falls into bed.

He lies on a bed without sheets. It's too hot for sheets, too hot for talking, but his wife lying next to him insists on talking.

"It wasn't your fault. It wasn't mine either. You know the

shitty way we got together. Bob saw in me the woman that *I* saw in me. He didn't judge. He didn't call me trash. I'm sorry but you judged. I don't know what happened to us, but when Bob touched me, I felt like *me* again. I want you to understand. I just want you to understand."

It's too hot for sheets, and she won't shut up about Bob.

The hunter pulls the pillow over his face. "Just when things are getting better," he whispers. In his farcical voice he adds, *"Oh, Bob, you're gonna get it."*

"I want you to understand. I just want you to understand," she says.

The Baby

It is the third night later. They have been drinking beers.

It is 10:00 p.m.

"The baby's name when it's born shall be Xavier," the hunter says.

"Bobette," says his wife, "if it's a girl."

"Bitch."

She kicks at him in the bed, laughing. "I was just teasing. Get over it."

They are tipsy from drinking beers. The hunter is a light-weight who doesn't drink except with her. She is pregnant, and she should not drink. When she drinks, she says crazy things. But *this* thing? No.

He turns on the lamp by the bed, and the veins in his face are so red they're popping. "If you weren't pregnant."

"If I weren't pregnant, *what?*"

He chooses his words with care: "I would fucking kill you."

The Tit

Supporting her enormous belly with her hands, the hunter's wife struggles to a sitting position, then struggles to her feet. She changes into her pregnant jeans, a *Powerpuff Girls* T-shirt, and her throwback Converse sneakers. She walks to the closet and takes out the small red suitcase that is always packed and ready for the hospital, sets it on the bed, and throws in an extra shirt and two panties.

"Where are you going?" he says. "To Bob's?"

She holds up her middle finger. "Kiss my ass." Even if she were going to Bob's, does he really think she would tell him? Anyway, she can't go to Bob's anymore. After the beating Bob took, the man wants no part of her. He tells her so each time they speak. And that's okay, she doesn't love Bob, never loved him, but it's nice to talk. Truth be told, the fear in Bob's voice, the jumpiness, warms her up for the hunter, who is by far the better lover. Without looking at him, she says, "I was just kidding, but you're a real asshole. I'm going to Mom's."

"Trash among trash," he says.

"Fuck you," she says.

"You're not taking the kids."

"You're the better parent, of course."

"Damn right I'm better."

She rolls her eyes. "Of course you are." She tosses two more pregnancy T-shirts into the suitcase and slams it closed. She opens it again and throws in the panties Bob likes, slams it closed again. She walks to the door where she cries a little. She wipes her face with her T-shirt and blows her nose in it. *Trash*. She slumps against the door, waiting for him to apologize. She waits more than a minute. The waiting hurts. She speaks before turning around. "Xena," she says. "Xena, if it's a girl."

"That's a good name," he says, reaching for the lamp beside the bed, turning it off. "You know I would never hurt you."

"You're mean."

"You started it."

"You're still mean."

In the darkness, she returns the suitcase to the closet. She undresses silently and comes back to bed. He touches the baby bump, and she slaps his face.

"Okay," he says. "I deserved that."

Later, when she begins to snore, he gets up from the bed and picks up from the floor the *Powerpuff Girls* T-shirt she blew her nose in and takes it into the bathroom where he sets it in the sink and lets it run under the faucet. Then he drops it in the rickety washing machine where it will wait until tomorrow. If he washes it tonight, the noise might wake the children.

—In the morning, he rolls over in the bed to find her not there. In the children's room, it's the same. Empty.

"She took the kids," he says out loud. "She'll be back."

He's the better parent. At least they agree on that. He does all the cooking, all the cleaning, all the washing, all the sitting up with them when they're sick.

But he waits all day and they do not return.

Just as it's getting dark, he calls his favorite journalist.

"I'm away from my desk right now. Please leave a message at the sound of the tone."

"I just wanted to talk, but I guess you're away from your desk. A lot of things are happening. I am a tormented soul." He slams down the phone and curses. He really wanted to talk.

Ten hours they've been out. Ten hours.

—At the eleventh hour, he hears a key in the door. Eleven hours they were gone.

She says, "Honey, we're home."

Junior says, "We brought pizza!"

He's prepared to continue the fight, if that's what she wants. Or to apologize, if that's what she wants. He's on the settee with his back to the door. He hears it shut. He hears Junior again, "Pizza!" And Zoe now, "Pizza." He senses her behind him. He feels the warmth of her body when she kisses the top of his head.

"I'm sorry," he says.

"You'd better be," she says.

She leans over his shoulder, puts her face next to his. He slides a hand into her shirt and feels her tit. They both laugh.

2003

Cassidy

The baby is a boy. They named him Xavier, and another is on the way.

In 2003, money is tight. With Junior, Zoe, Xavier, and the other on the way, they struggle to make the rent. Household expenses, utilities, food for the kids, gas for the old Buick, her tuition at the community college—where does it all go?

The hunter's wife teaches music at the community center. She has private students who come to the house. She works at her best friend's family's funeral home, but it's not enough.

At the restaurant, the hunter is promoted from assistant manager to manager, but it's not enough, and though now he is one step below Vince, he complains about being taken off the road where he earns the biggest tips among the drivers, tips bigger than his salary as a manager.

Vince Muncie, the owner of Munchie Luciano's, a six-table restaurant and pizzeria that's been in business since 1962, is the big boss. He makes all the decisions. He's got three younger brothers and a sister, all of whom inherited a share of the business from their father Bruno, but Vince is who chose the uniform—the midnight-black T-shirt with a topping of pepperoni clusters dotting the sleeves—because he's the big boss. The black van with no markings, just a magnetic sign that attaches to the roof when you're delivering, easily removed when you're done, when you're done it looks like any ordinary black van—all of that was decided by Vince, the big boss. Vince understands that the hunter, his manager and most loyal employee, needs the tips to survive, so he allows him to make a few deliveries each night among his other assigned duties. The hunter is also on standby duty. If a driver is reluctant to deliver to one of the less reputable neighborhoods, the hunter will go. His pressed T-shirt, neat haircut, polished work shoes, and friendly smile mask a terrifying fierceness. He has never been successfully robbed, and there have been attempts. After one such event, Vince asked him about it.

"Never bring a gun to a knife fight," the hunter had said, stroking his chin like a philosopher.

"I see what you're saying," said Vince, nodding in agreement.

Vince, the big boss, had no idea what his best employee meant.

—The hunter hires on as an overnight security guard at the mall. He can pay the bills now, but when can he hunt? He finds the situation ironic. A second job should make hunting easier, as it allows an excuse to be out all night. If he could just slip away—but his new boss is a real ball buster. His new boss docks him for going fifteen minutes over his break. For fifteen minutes, he loses an hour of minimum wage.

With his wife pregnant again, the urge grows stronger. It starts interfering with his job. He confuses NW with NE. He loses his way on familiar streets. He arrives at deliveries without the pizza. In the kitchen, mistakes are made as well. The dough is overly thick, or overly thin. Sometimes it lands on the floor. He can't focus. Then the thing with the short customer happens.

He comes in for a pickup order, a dark-haired, handsome man in a blue and red plaid shirt. He is short, no taller than

5'7". He is a loudmouth, and he's had too much to drink. They get into a yelling fight over the wrong change, and the loudmouth, who believes the hunter is constrained by the decorum implicit in his job, flings a ketchup packet at him. It's not even close. The hunter's fingers must be pried from his blue-veined throat.

The short customer threatens to sue. Vince bribes him with free pizza for a year and he agrees to drop it.

"It's only small change after all. Let him keep it," the short customer says.

"You keep it, you lying bastard," the hunter says, and flips the small change at the short man's face. A buck fifty in quarters, one quarter at a time.

Vince suspends him for a month.

The Baby

"The baby's name when it is born shall be Vincent," says the hunter's wife.

"Vanessa," says the hunter, "if it's a girl."

The New Van

At home he is a nuisance, cleaning and cooking in a frenzy, constantly rubbing his wife's stomach and saying: "It feels like a girl. You think it's a girl?" If she complains or even looks at him wrong, he explodes. "This one's mine, right? Then I'll rub it any damn time I please. Is that a problem?"

It's too much. He can't fight it. He needs to hunt.

He quits his job in the mall, and he stalks the bastard who lied about the small change. The bastard's name is Cassidy Sanders, a mattress salesman. Cassidy. Like Butch Cassidy—Butch Cassidy is a dead man too.

He follows Cassidy to a nightclub and catches him in the act.

He's a handsome guy. He could get them to sleep with him without doping their drinks. He does it because he's a bastard. Cassidy is gonna get it.

But the hunter's wife miscarries.

—Broken toys. Bad dreams. Dead goldfish. All of it. Children are precious.

Despite his grief, the hunter is determined. He will hunt the small-change-stealing, date-raping bastard regardless.

At another nightclub, he watches the bastard drop the powder into another woman's drink. The hunter curses under his breath as the drug works its transformative magic on her—the slurred speech, the head lolling to one side as the hallucinations set in. She leaves the nightclub groggy on

Cassidy's arm, destined to find herself in a compromising position, consenting while not consenting. Of course, she will not remember his name when asked by the police, if she goes to the police. She will remember only that he was cute, a bit on the short side, and seemed like a nice guy.

The hunter is familiar with that kind of dope. He used it on Eduardo and had planned to use it on all the dead men until he calculated the expense.

Cassidy uses it on women. Cassidy's gonna get it.

The hunter saves his tips for a month, buys some of the good stuff from his connection. It is the same stuff Cassidy uses, ketamine, though in a more potent mix that knocks you straight out.

His connection warns him: "A little bit more and it could kill the girl."

"It's not for a girl," the hunter says. "It's for a rat."

—The next night a misty rain falls.

The hunter follows Cassidy's brand-new Honda Accord into the parking lot of a Publix grocery store on West 49th. He parks alongside the dead man's car and slides open the side panel. The car is a beauty, with all the toys. Sunroof. Windows with a chrome trim. Leather-wrapped steering wheel. It's a shame to leave behind such a beautiful car. But he's a rapist and a loudmouth.

Cassidy exits his car. The hunter watches with the windows down, taking the measure of the man. Cassidy does a little hop to avoid stepping into a pothole. He waddles when he walks. There is something wrong with one of his legs. He is short and doesn't weigh much, maybe 150, maybe 160. Cassidy is not obese according to the charts. The hunter slips a stick of gum into his mouth.

The automatic doors of the Publix fan open and the smug

loudmouth bastard walks inside. The hunter will get him when he returns to his car. People are less cautious on the way to their car after grocery shopping. Trying to remember if they bought everything on their list. Digging around in their pocket for keys. Recalling where they parked.

He will slap a hand over Cassidy's small-change-stealing, date-raping mouth, jab him in the neck with a dose of his own medicine, and hold him up until his body goes limp. Then he will heft him into the open side panel of the van and set him down on the clean mattress in the back. No doubt the dead man will awaken before they get to the spot in the Everglades where his body parts will be dumped. He will struggle to break free from the leather straps holding his arms and legs in place. His scream will die in the towel stuffed in his mouth. When he comes to his senses and realizes there is no way out, that his fate is sealed, he and the hunter will discuss mattresses. The hunter will have to do all the talking because of the towel in the dead man's mouth.

A few minutes later, Cassidy emerges from the store pushing a cart with a ten-pound sack of dog food, a gallon of bottled water, three long-stemmed sunflowers, and other groceries in brown paper bags. Huddled under an umbrella with him is one of his doping victims from the nightclub, a doe-eyed, slim-hipped woman in a green Publix uniform.

He date rapes her and now they are a couple? Unbelievable. The hunter swears an oath as the misty rain falls. *You're gonna get it, Cassidy. You can bet on that.*

The black van roars out of the parking lot.

—He almost grabs him coming home from the mattress store on 57th in Hialeah where he's the top salesman, but they make eye contact, and she is there. Cassidy makes a face at him and gets into her car. He almost grabs Cassidy from the gym at the Waterways where he works out, but she is there too, working out. He almost grabs him in a crowd at South Beach, but she is there. Cassidy regularly comes in for his free pizza, but guess who's with him? The doe-eyed girl is always there.

Then Vince, the big boss, trades in the old Ford panel van for a newer van, a Dodge that has an air bag, reclining seats, and a side panel that rises when a button on the dashboard is pushed.

"Damn," the hunter says.

He waits to see if the new owner of the old van spots something, some piece of evidence that he may have left behind. A drop of blood on a piece of fabric torn from a shirt; a curl of old skin in the tight creases in the seats. Will there come the heavy pounding on the door by the police? Or their sudden appearance at the restaurant, guns drawn?

A month passes, and no cops.

Well, of course they find nothing, because the hunter has left nothing behind to be found. The hunter is a perfectionist, his cleaning immaculate.

The old mattress fits perfectly. The new van is larger, more capacious. He prepares it for the hunt, but bad news like blind mice comes in threes.

First, the miscarriage. Then Vince trades in the van. Now this: Cassidy is packing up to leave the state.

—From the shadows, the hunter watches the moving van as the movers pack Cassidy's modernist couch, his rattan wardrobe, his king-size bed frame, his king-size mattress. Cassidy in his brand-new Honda drives behind the moving van as he relocates to Nebraska. The doe-eyed girl never leaves his side.

The hunter follows their car as far as Tallahassee, going through four packs of peppermint gum, before giving up.

* * *

—On New Year's Eve, he calls his favorite journalist to wish her a happy new year.

"*I'm away from my desk right now. Please leave a message at the sound of the tone.*"

The hunter says, "Should auld acquaintance be forgot and never brought to mind? I just wanted to talk, but I guess you're away from your desk."

—In his notes he writes, *All in all, 2003 was a wasted year. The rat got away. At least the wife is pregnant again.*

The Baby

"The baby's name when it is born shall be Victor," says the hunter's wife.

"Venus," says the hunter, "if it's a girl."

2004

The Snatcher

Since 1992, South Florida has been terrorized by a serial killer targeting children of color.

The perpetrator behind what has become known as the Snatch Murders is responsible for the abduction and murder of at least four children between the ages of nine and ten. Three more deaths are still being investigated for possible inclusion in this grisly death toll.

The pattern is the same in each case. The children are taken from a public place like a park or a shopping center. A week to ten days after the abduction, the parents receive a letter posted through the US Mail from a person calling himself "Snatcher."

The effect of the note—rendered in purple crayon in a child's careful script—is chilling. Before telling the parents where the child's body can be found, it begins with the horrifying four-word direct address: I'm in heaven Mommy.

One body was found seated on a park bench, another hidden in a tree house on property that had been seized in foreclosure, one floating in the drainage ditch behind the popular children's restaurant and bounce-house, Rob E. Rabbit's. Ten-year-old Maryanne Jamison was found in a sleeping bag left on a coconut palm tree–shaded footpath at Crandon Park Beach. Each child was found clutching a white lily.

Jermaine Milkovich, age 10, has been missing since Wednesday, July 7. By all indications, Jermaine, the Miami Shores fourth grader with the sunny smile who loves baseball and Sonic the Hedgehog *video games, might be a Snatcher victim. If so, he would be the Snatcher's first victim since Maryanne Jamison in 1999.*

Police believe there is still hope because the parents haven't yet received a note from the Snatcher telling them where Jermaine's body can be found.

If you have any information, contact your local police department or sheriff's office.

To the Snatcher, we have included a note from Jermaine's parents pleading to you for their child's release:

We are Jermaine's Mommy and Daddy. Please return Jermaine to us. We miss Jermaine and love him very much. Please tell Jermaine that we love him. God bless you, sir.

—Heidi Renoir-Smith, *Miami Herald*

Carl

Eduardo and David are mostly forgotten until he reads the second article by Heidi Renoir-Smith: "When Will He Strike Again?"

Heidi Renoir-Smith's articles may be sensational but they are well researched and mostly unbiased. In her latest article, she got it right in the specific details of her sensationalized report.

Yes, there was a call two days later at 10:00 p.m. informing the authorities where the bodies could be found. Yes, the body parts were found dumped in the Everglades in three separate butcher sacks: head and torso in one; arms in another; legs in the final one. The authorities thought they could get a lead by tracing the butcher sacks back to the meat markets and butcher shops that owned them, but the hunter was too clever for that. He had done the butcher sack break-ins in three separate Florida cities.

Eduardo Gomez: West Palm Beach, Homestead, Tallahassee.

David Perez: Ocala, Miami Beach, South Bay.

. . . the clock is ticking. Over the past six months, butcher sacks have been reported stolen in Hialeah and Ft. Lauderdale. Last month in the city of Valdosta, which is located in the southern part of Georgia near its border with Florida, a butcher sack was sto-

len. Law enforcement believes that this is the third and final sack in the ritual of the murderer who they are calling the Periwinkle Killer, or Periwinkle. Is the Periwinkle Killer ready to strike again? Is there a connection between the Periwinkle Killer and the Snatcher, two murderers whose rituals involve flowers?

Heidi got that part wrong. The hunter would never work with the Snatcher. He would chop the Snatcher's lungs. He would sever the Snatcher's limbs. He would bag him and pack him. He would disappear the Snatcher in the swamp. The hunter is hunting again because his wife is pregnant again.

It is Sunday evening, and she calls him into the bathroom to show him the sticky fluid on the floor.

"My water broke."

The hunter grabs the kids and the packed suitcase.

The kids he drops off at his mother's. The packed suitcase he carries to the hospital along with his pregnant wife.

—At the hospital, the nurse informs them that their obstetrician, Dr. Sara Wayman, is at a conference in Cincinnati, so they will have to use Dr. Carlito Pabón, who is young but has excellent skills.

"Let's see what we have here." Dr. Carlito Pabón, his eyes squinting behind thick-rimmed glasses, places the stethoscope on her chest between her breasts. He fits his fingers into blue plastic gloves and puts his hand on her stomach. He moves it around, feeling for something. His face knits up. He frowns, he smiles. He has her spread her legs and investigates her vagina with a small silver flashlight. It is cold to the touch and she shivers. He lifts his head and says, "It's going to be a long labor."

"Okay," the hunter says.

"Okay," says his wife.

Dr. Pabón wears a stethoscope and a bushy mustache to distract from his youthfulness. "How many do you have already? Children, I mean."

"Three," they say together, beaming. "Junior, Zoe Yasmine, and Xavier William."

"This one makes four?"

"He's hoping for another girl, Venus," the hunter's wife says.

"We'll settle for Victor if it's a boy," the hunter says.

"I wanted to name it Brian if it was a boy and Judy, after my sister, if it was a girl, but he said the name has to begin with a V. It's crazy, I know, but I owe him. He's a good daddy," the hunter's wife explains.

"Oh, I see," says the doctor, lifting his eyes, "they're in alphabetical order."

"What?" says the wife.

"Z, Y, X, W, V."

"What do you mean?" she says.

Dr. Pabón, who is only half listening now, grunts dismissively and walks over to a small trash can in the corner of the room and steps on the foot pedal. When the lid pops open, he pulls off the blue plastic gloves and drops them inside.

Despite the stethoscope and white coat, Dr. Pabón could be a kid. Not much more than 5'7". Shave the mustache, he'd be the spitting image of Bryce. The grunt? The hunter does not take an offense to his wife lightly, and the young doctor has offended her by brushing her off. He could cancel Carl Graham, whom he has been stalking six months, and pencil in Dr. Carlito Pabón.

No.

He would have to start from scratch. The six months on

Carl Graham would be wasted, and he'd have another six months to go. Furthermore, killing a second doctor and a third Cuban would further confuse them. He needs them to pay attention so he can throw them off his tail thinking he's crazy. He's not crazy. He's got a plan.

"You'd better watch out, Doctor," he says under his breath.

"Watch what?" his wife says.

"Nothing," the hunter says. He does not take his eyes off Dr. Pabón, who scratches something on his pad and leaves the room.

His wife watches his eyes following Dr. Pabón. "Honey?" she says.

"Nothing." He takes her hand. "Nothing at all."

She accepts this answer. Why shouldn't she? She's just as clueless as the authorities. Of course he alphabetized the kids. He alphabetized the dead men too. Eduardo, David, Carl. How much easier must he make it for them?

Since there is to be a long labor, the hunter rests in a chair beside the bed while his wife slowly turns pages in a magazine, *Pregnancy Today*, that was left in the room. All is quiet but for the electronic beeping of hospital machinery and the chatter of two brown orderlies in the hall:

"You talk to Betty yet?"

"Which one she is?"

"The one who work in the OR."

"Yeah, mon. Gal got dem pretty leg."

The hunter stretches his long legs and closes his eyes.

—At 8:17 p.m., Dada appears behind him and speaks.

Son.

The hunter can see his father without turning, so he knows that he has fallen asleep. In dreams, he can see his father no matter where he stands—before him, behind him, by his side.

Carl is ready.

I'm on my way, the hunter answers without speaking. Then he opens his eyes. He tells his wife, "I've got to check in at the restaurant."

The magazine rustles as she lowers it. "But I'm in labor."

"A *long* labor," he reminds. "This will be quick. Two hours at the most."

"Two hours? Don't you dare leave—"

But the hunter is already out of the room.

—Carl lives in an apartment building in a broken and irreparable part of Palmetto Cove, a neighborhood of crumbling walls, streetlights that don't work, and alleys that stink of dog manure and homeless piss.

Carl is smallish, about 5'7", but well formed. He lives here with his two older brothers, both of whom are big-bodied men employed as enforcers in the illegal drug trade. Unlike them, Carl teaches piano to nine- and ten-year-old boys.

Carl drives a late-model Toyota, ash-gray with silver trim. Yesterday the passenger seat was occupied by a weeping brown boy of ten, or was he nine? Carl dried the boy's tears, kissed him on the mouth one more time, and promised that it wouldn't happen again.

"I'll tell your mom you're making progress," Carl said to the boy, "or I can tell her that you liked it. You're not a sissy, right?"

The hunter didn't hear these words. He only saw the struggling boy. The kiss.

Carl is a dead man.

He almost took Carl yesterday, but his big-bodied brothers hadn't left town yet. Carl is a monster that preys on children. Even so, the pain the hunter is going to inflict on Carl has nothing to do with that.

Well, almost nothing.

The hunter loves children.

Pablum and shoelaces; first crushes and cartoons; the measles, the mumps, boogers, goddamn it—all of it!

—Carl ascends the stairs to his second-floor apartment. The hunter follows a mere five steps behind. The hallway is carpeted, and his footfalls are light, but the hunter knows that if Carl turns, he will see him—a lowly pizza man carrying a pizza-warmer bag on his shoulder. If Carl turns, the hunter will walk away. The hunter will return to the hospital to his wife who is about to give birth to a child named Victor if it's a boy or Venus if it's a girl.

Carl will live another day if he turns. Dada taught him the beauty of surprise: *The shocked look on their faces— you will enjoy that. It is essential that your work bring you joy. The hunt can be difficult. There is the considerable investment of labor and time, time that could be better spent with your family, and there is the money—the cost of gas and tools. There is always the danger of getting caught, of course. It's worthless without the joy.*

Carl will live another day if he turns, but he doesn't turn. Instead he inserts the key in the lock, twists the knob, and opens the door. The hunter shoves him inside and the warmer bag falls, spilling the knives. The hunter catches the rapier before it hits the ground.

Carl swings around with a snub-nosed revolver in his hand, but he hesitates and the hunter bats the gun aside and sinks the blade in his ribs.

—He holds Carl up until most of the life has seeped from his body. Then he gently places him on the hardwood floor and leaves to get the rest of his equipment from the van. Out of force of habit, he's quick about it, but he has time enough. In a dream, his father told him that Carl's brothers would not return for a week.

His own stalking of the dead man confirmed it.

—The hunter returns to the apartment with the tools. He sets them down and waits on the piano bench for Carl to drain out.

Aside from teaching children of the poor, Carl performs at churches. Last week, the hunter attended one of his performances. As much as he hates him, Carl is a fine musician, one of the best the hunter has ever heard.

Watching Carl die on the floor, the hunter is compelled to ask: "Why did you hesitate? Why didn't you just shoot me?"

Carl has lost so much blood his voice is low, and the hunter must position his ear near the man's chalk-pale lips in order to hear.

"The flowers fell from your pocket. You're him, right?"

"I am he."

"The Periwinkle Killer. You're a pizza man?"

A sly smile creeps across the hunter's face as he checks Carl's pulse.

"They think we're monsters, but we're not. You're the hero in your story, I'm the hero in mine," Carl says. Mustering a breath, he pleads: "I can't help it, I have urges. I didn't mean to hurt the children."

"That's not what this is about," the hunter says. He slips a stick of peppermint gum in his mouth, though there is already a piece in there.

Carl gathers what strength he has left. "Then tell me what it's about!"

The hunter jams the blade in his throat, silencing him.

KILLER
INCHOATE

Palmetto Grove Senior High

There was a girl.

Mary Eugenia Fisk.

And Bryce decided that he and the hunter should join the Science Club to show off their talents and get into good colleges.

The two ninth-grade best friends had no scientific talent whatsoever and no reason to be numbered among that coterie of elite children. Their grasp of understanding in all areas of science was less than average.

Bryce, however, was a genius where calculations in math were involved—he could trace evidence to conclusion, and conclusion back to evidence. The nerds accepted his "trick" as science and welcomed him into their exclusive clique.

As for *his* "trick," the hunter, who was good at noting things, could recite upon command the electron configuration of every element on the periodic table. Never mind that he knew not what to do with that knowledge. He impressed the nerds by spouting random, inane, rubbish phrasings that included an obscure element or two and gained acceptance into their community of talented outcasts.

Mary Eugenia Fisk was in that group as well, and she was just as useless to the scientific community as were the hunter and Bryce.

In the Science Club photos freshman year, Bryce's handsome tanned face is all angles under a helmet of wavy black hair. At 5'7", he is a tad under average in stature but well above average in physique. His body is a perfect swimmer's V, for he is on the swim team—and the baseball team and the soccer team and the football team.

Bryce is not obese at all.

—Mary Eugenia Fisk stands between her best friend the gawky girl Tina and the nerd called "Muscle Teeth." She is so tall she leans, but hers is not an uneasy height. She is statuesque—with curves like a fashion model, which is to say, almost no curves, though what curves there be do beckon. If she were smaller, she'd be called *pixie-like*.

Mary Eugenia Fisk is much too pretty to be a nerd, though her prettiness is precisely why she was welcomed into Science Club. Some nerds are blind to beauty, but not all, and Mary knows that she is beautiful.

On this picture day, Mary Eugenia Fisk wears two lipsticks, Rock-'Em-Sock-'Em Yellow and Go-Team-Go Blue. She is an athlete. She plays girls' basketball and is also on the tennis team. In fact, she holds a tennis racket in her left hand. Did she forget that this is Science Club? Is that a smile or a smirk?

Mary Eugenia Fisk is wise beyond her years.

The eyes of Mary Eugenia Fisk are a gray that sparkles blue. She wears her magnificent bronze hair pulled back tight on her head on this picture day. In the future, the hunter will see it in a French braid. He will see it in twin ponytails with black ribbons. He will see it decorated with flowers. In the future when they are married, he will see it dyed black, cut short, and worn in a pixie bob.

—There are two photos of the hunter in the ninth grade.

In the first one, he stands alone—a monstrosity with a long, pale face, freckles, and a crooked smile. His eyes are black as a starless midnight. His long-fingered hands clutch a science textbook as gray and tattered as the noble garments that hang from his anorexic frame. If photographs possessed smell and taste, his would smell of ashes and taste of dust. He's hunched over. He's a walking skeleton with a twisted spine.

He's a five-hundred-year-old teenager fresh from the grave. He's Nosferatu.

—He's Count Dracula.

In the second photo, his outfit is varying shades of gray, from his name-brand sneakers to his stylish overcoat and anachronistic ascot. His outfit is composed of expensive and often clashing elements indicative of his family's nobility and his own vanity.

In this group shot, he stands apart from the rest. His eyes are vacant, his skin pale, for he is dead. He is a corpse who struts with flair.

In the photograph, he stares out at you. He's arrogant, and he loathes you.

You are mere mortal. He is the ancient evil.

—The other students say he is a fright in these Science Club photographs, and he would agree. In the photographs, you are seeing the hunter as the hunter once saw himself. Behold the killer inchoate. Behold the monster in his infancy. A photograph is future memory.

—Ah, if only it were true.

The truth is that in ninth grade the hunter does not wear an ascot, nor does he own expensive sneakers. He possesses an overcoat, but it is drab olive and fur-lined for Miami's fickle winters, six hot days, one suddenly cold. Army-navy surplus and Goodwill, that is all that his impoverished mother can afford since his father went away.

The truth is that he is shy. He is timid. He dresses so as to remain invisible, and you'd be hard-pressed to see him in the Science Club photos. He feigned illness on picture day and stayed at home setting rattraps.

An emaciated Nosferatu? Hardly.

The truth is that the hunter before he was the hunter was a chubby, freckle-faced, fatherless boy named Poe Edgar.

Oh, how Poe wishes he had owned an ascot and eccentric clothes and expensive sneakers in ninth grade.

He wishes they had had money when he was in ninth grade. He wishes that his dada had not gone away.

All he can do is stare at the space in the yearbook where his photograph would have been and wish he had been normal.

Ten to Two

There was a girl.

Andrea Stewart.

Bryce had so many girls it was hard to keep track of whom he was kissing or not kissing from week to week—but this Andrea.

"I want you to call her for me."

"Why me?" Poe said.

"You're my best friend."

"Thrilling," Poe said in a droll voice, but his heart raced whenever Bryce said they were best friends. Bryce was a real good best friend. Bryce always had his back.

"I'm busted," Bryce said. He explained that Andrea had caught him kissing another girl, Jessica, by the water fountain outside the gym and dumped him.

But what did he expect Poe to do about it? High school drama annoyed Poe, he didn't know anything about girls, and he didn't know Andrea, didn't even know what she looked like though she sat behind him in English.

"Of course you know her," Bryce insisted. "You guys are so much alike. You have the same kind of logic mixed with craziness. She'll believe it coming from you."

For a moment, Poe reflected on the way other people viewed him. His odd sense of humor. His strange, spiraling laugh. *Tehehe.* The nerd among nerds.

"Does she even know I exist?" Poe said.

"She talks about you all the time. She says you're smart

and you seem trustworthy. Tell her I'm sorry I cheated."

"I'll tell her you're sorry . . . that you got caught."

"Come on, dude. I'm serious. Call her, tell her I'm sorry. I'll be waiting by the phone."

"You'll be waiting by the phone for *me?* How nice. Bryce, Bryce, Bryce."

"That's not my name. Stop being weird."

"Bryce, Bryce, Bryce. Tehehe."

2

When she picked up, it was exactly 10:00 p.m.

"Who is this?"

"Poe. Poe Jackson."

"Gerardo's weird friend," she said in a voice that was low and bluesy. "He told you to call?"

"He said he's sorry he cheated. He said if you would but take him back, he'll make you his one and only."

"If I *would but* take him back? Did you just say *would but*?"

"Yes."

"Who talks that way?"

"I do."

"Are you Shakespeare?"

"I'm me."

"Hmm. Well, who are *you*?"

"Me," Poe said. When Andrea responded with a tired sigh, he said, "He promised he'd be true to you this time."

"I bet."

"He seems sincere," Poe said.

"That's his charm. *Seeming*."

"Give him another chance."

"No."

"Please."

"Not gonna do it."

"I'll split the fee with you if you would but take him back."

"The fee?"

"The finder's fee."

"The lost-and-finder's fee?"

"The lost-and-*founder's* fee."

"Ah," she said. "The you-lost-her-but-I-found-her fee?"

"I found her?"

"You found *me*."

"Tehehe."

"Hahaha. You're funny," she said wonderingly. "You always seem so serious."

"Not weird?"

"Not weird." She said, "We've gone to the same school since kindergarten, and this is the first time we've spoken."

"Bryce says you talk about me endlessly."

"I do not."

"Well, that's what Bryce says."

"Who?"

"Gerardo."

"Did you just call him Bryce?"

"Yes."

"Why do you call him Bryce?"

"Why *not* Bryce?"

"But why Bryce?"

"You don't think Bryce is a good name for him?" Poe said.

"I do not," Andrea said. "A better name for him would be *cad*."

"He's a cad?"

"He's a cad."

"Not a knave?"

"He's a knave too," she said. "The knave of hearts."

"Tehehe."

"Hahaha."

Behind her, there was a television playing suspenseful music then gunshots. A cop show was on. The channel switched to the sound of cheering. It was some kind of sports show now.

"I gotta go," she said.

"But—"

An agitated male voice talked loudly behind her.

"He needs to use the phone," she said. "Give me your number. I'll call you back."

Poe quickly gave her his number, and she was gone.

3

He liked her.

This was the first time that he liked someone other than Bryce. Well, he had liked his babysitter. But he was seven and she was sixteen. What boy doesn't have a crush on his babysitter? He liked Andrea too. He wondered what that meant.

"You are fascinating, Andrea," he said when she called back. It was fifteen minutes later and behind her it was quiet. The television noise had gone away. "Tell me about yourself."

"You first," she said.

"Ladies first," he said.

"Boys first," she said.

"Tehehe. If you *would but* go first, then I shall follow."

"Hahaha. Okay." She cleared her throat. "My name is Andrea Tierra Stewart."

"Tierra is a pretty name."

"My mother wanted to name me Tiara."

"Tiaras are pretty."

"The nurse who recorded it spoke Spanish and misunderstood. Oh, I guess Mom could've corrected it when she saw it in writing, but it was only a middle name."

"And a pretty name at that."

"That's what they said Mom said. She said it's wrong, but it's so pretty. She may have been in pain. I never knew her. She never left the hospital."

"Sorry."

Whoever had been in the room with her was gone now. When she told him her story, she spoke freely and without whispers. She was raised by her father and her grandparents, her mother's parents.

"Grandma's a photographer. Not the news kind, the artistic kind. Her photos are in art magazines and museums."

Poe was not into art, but he made a note to look up her grandmother's art photos.

"Granddad is an architect. He designed most of the houses in Palmetto Cove."

Poe wondered if Andrea's grandfather had designed his house. He made a note to look it up. The plan was for her father and mother to live with her grandparents until they got on their feet. Andrea's parents met in college. They were going to be teachers, but then her mother died giving birth to her. Nevertheless, when Andrea spoke, she was upbeat.

"My dad eventually got remarried and moved my stepmother into my grandparents' house. Isn't that unusual? I think it's about me. My dad's not Jewish, but they are. They wanted to keep their only grandchild close. I have three sisters: Jade, Pearl, and Trinket. And I was supposed to be Tiara, get it? They are my half sisters, actually, but I don't think of them as that. We get along real well—"

"Blah, blah, blah," he interrupted her. "Tell me about yourself. Your dad is a great guy. You granddad is a great guy. Your grandma is a great woman. Your sisters are great. Your mother, God bless the dead, was a great woman. Blah, blah, blah. Who is Andrea Tierra Stewart? I want to hear about *her*."

"I am what I am a part of. I am a part of my family, so I tell you about my family when you ask me about me," she said.

"Sad."

"I don't think it's sad."

"So sad."

"I have a 4.0 GPA. I play flute in the marching band."

"Sad. Sad."

"I plan to major in architecture in college."

"Like good old Granddad?"

"Yes."

"Sad."

"I'm ambidextrous."

"Sad."

"I can recite the alphabet backward."

"Interesting."

"What? That I can recite the alphabet backward?"

"Yes. Interesting. But it's all so sad, Andrea. I want to know your *mind*. I want to know your thoughts." Were they dark like his? Did she hear voices that spoke to her at night? Did they tell her to kill small animals? This was important, but he should not have quipped: "No wonder Bryce has looked to other girls for affection. Tehehe."

There was a sharp gasp from the other side.

"I shouldn't have said that."

No answer came from the other side. It had only been a joke. He didn't know anything about girls. He had ruined it.

"Andrea."

Again no answer.

"Andrea, I'm sorry I said that. If you would but accept my apology—"

She hung up.

He clutched the phone in his hand, the silent receiver pressed desperately to his face. What can you say to a girl? What can you *not* say to a girl? He knew nothing about girls, nothing at all. Bryce was waiting by the phone. Poe had to call him, but what would he tell him? He began to dial, pausing after each digit he touched, but then he stopped.

He would call *her* instead.

3-0-5-6-2-1 . . .

4

She picked up on the first ring.

"You're probably right. I'm boring, I'm too smart, I'm too stupid, I'm too self-aware, I'm too self-unaware, I'm too much of a nerd."

"I didn't mean it like that. I don't know how to talk to girls, is all."

"But it's true anyway," she said, "and that's why you're not going to collect your lost-and-found-her fee."

"What?" he said. "Oh!"

"Hahaha."

"Tehehe."

Music began to play behind her. "*I'll be your lover, whenever, forever.*" The song was popular on the radio. Was it coming from a radio? Was it coming from her CD player? If it was coming from her CD player, did she choose that song for *him?*

"*Just say you want me. Whenever, forever.*"

"Now you," she said.

"Did you play that song because—?"

"*I'll be your lover, whenever, forever.*"

"No. That's the radio. I'll turn it down," she said, over the music. She turned it down, but not off. "Now you," she repeated. "Tell me about yourself, Mister Smarty Pants."

"*Whenever, forever.*"

"I'm a closed book," he said.

"Open the book, or tell Bryce it's over."

"I made you call him Bryce."

"It fits him," she said. "Now talk."

"Chapter One," he said. "I know the electron configuration of every element on the periodic table."

"Sad."

"I collect rats."

"Like Ben?"

"Who?"

"Michael Jackson. Ben. The song from the movie *Ben*. Ben is a pet rat."

"Oh," he said, wondering who Ben was. But a rat? "It's like Ben, then. Yes."

"Sad."

"Okay," he said. "My name was given to me by my deceased father."

"I'm sorry."

"God bless the dead."

"God bless the dead," she said.

"My father's name was Edgar L. Jackson. His favorite writer was Edgar Allan Poe. So I am Poe Edgar Jackson. Poe Jackson, to you."

"Interesting."

"You think so?"

"Actually, it's kinda creepy," she said.

"My dad was a creepy guy," he said. "Tehehe."

The song was "I'll Be Your Lover" by the R&B group III Handsome Men, and it returned several times on the radio as they traded jokes and secrets well into the night. Their banter was easy as though they had been friends their entire lives. Of course, he did not ask her to describe what she looked like. How embarrassing it would be to admit that he had no idea who he was talking to.

He had a vague notion of a heart-shaped face, dark

hair, and dark eyes. Soft and motherly, like Mary in the Bible.

A half-Jewish girl.

5

Finally, at 2:00 a.m., the phone call came to an end. Bryce's name had appeared on the caller ID ten times within the first two hours of the marathon conversation.

"You're trying to steal my girl."

"She just kept talking. I didn't want to be rude."

"I was right. You guys do have a lot in common. Same sense of humor."

"And a dead parent."

"She has a dead parent?"

"Her mother," Poe says. "And she's Jewish."

"I never knew that. That can't be," Bryce said. He mulled this for a moment and then said: "Do you like her, or what?"

"Why would you ask that? She's sat behind me all year in English and I can't tell you what she looks like. What does she look like?"

"You already know. I'm not telling you."

"Come on, Bryce. What does she look like?"

"Stop calling me Bryce or I won't tell you."

"Bryce."

"Dufus."

But a half-Jewish girl with that voice and that wit? He revised his vision to frizzy blond hair, alert hazel eyes, and a small sad mouth with a wisecracking smile.

Like a young Barbra Streisand.

Ben

He didn't sleep until 5:00. When he awoke at 5:50, he felt completely rested.

He got up and went behind the house to check the rat-trap. There was a rat in it, injured, but still alive. He named him Ben.

Then he sliced off Ben's head, stomped him until he was flat, and tossed him like a Frisbee into the trash can.

Brown

In Mrs. Hanna's English class, they were seated in alphabetical order. As a "Stewart," she sat two rows behind him. He bustled in just before the late bell to get an unobstructed view of her. She was settling into her seat, having bustled in scant seconds ahead of him.

Yes, he had seen her before, and she was beautiful.

She was invisible only because she was brown, brown, brown, a brown girl with dull reddish-brown hair. Brown was not the color for him.

Her eyes were intelligent and brown also, with flecks of green and gold in them. She had a delicate nose. Her lips were surprisingly thin, and when they parted—ah, the flaw was unveiled in this portrait of brown comeliness. She wore braces. She was a brown-eyed girl with braces, and he tried to decide how he felt about this, and realized it was not a flaw—but Bryce, oh yes, Bryce.

She was Bryce's girl.

When he looked back, Andrea Tierra Stewart fastened those brown eyes on him. Her smile mouthed the words: *You're late. Hahaha.*

His smile mouthed back: *You're early. Tehehe.*

The fifty minutes of Mrs. Hanna's English could not pass fast enough. When the class ended, he went to her.

She said, "Finally, face-to-face."

He said, "I thought you said you were Jewish, but you're—"

"Black? Yes, my dad's black. Is that a problem?"

"No. Not at all."

"It better not be." She hooked his arm and they walked down the hall, picking up the conversation where it had left off the night before.

6

In the cafeteria, they sat with Bryce and three of his companions, Tipp, Tadd, and Muscle Teeth. Tipp and Tadd were Bryce's cool friends. The nerd they called Muscle Teeth possessed teeth that were flawless.

The other kids would say, "No cavities? As much candy as he eats, his teeth must lift weights. They must be on steroids. They must be muscle teeth."

Silly.

Poe had no fondness for Bryce's obnoxious friends, but Bryce had friends and Poe had none, so he borrowed Bryce's. In much the same way, Bryce had charisma. Poe had none, so he basked in Bryce's. Bryce was ever the center of attention. Poe would hang on his every word or on every word that was said about him, but not that day.

During the conversation that day, he missed some crucial thing that Bryce had said, and missing it failed to trouble him as it would have before Andrea.

In fact, Andrea, who was seated next to Bryce, but across from Poe, at times alluded to things they had said to each other the night before. When Bryce finally complained that he didn't get it, she told him, "I guess you just had to be there."

These words filled Poe with a mischievous delight.

Andrea

There were *three* couples, really: Bryce and Andrea; Andrea and Poe; Poe and Bryce. Looked at another way, Bryce and Andrea were a couple, and Poe was a brother to Bryce, but a brother to Andrea also.

For example, when Bryce cheated on Andrea with Jessica Sepulveda, a senior pretty enough to go out for homecoming queen, Andrea came to Poe, her *brother*, for comfort, and he comforted her.

Then she said, "I couldn't care less about him."

The Brother

When Jessica Sepulveda, the raven-haired, runner-up homecoming queen with the breathtaking emerald eyes, stole Bryce from her entirely, Andrea came to Poe, her *brother*, and said, "As long as I have you, I don't need a boyfriend."

They sat on her bed. Her room faced west, and the setting sun peeked through the slatted blinds. She touched the chain around his neck. "Can I wear it?"

He opened his mouth to say something. She read the look on his face and elbowed him playfully. "It's not like that. We're just friends."

Sad face.

"I'm not saying that it can't lead to something."

Happy face.

He took off the chain and hung it around her neck and started fumbling with the clasp. Maybe it was the slatted light in the room. Maybe it was the perfume of her skin. Maybe it was the touch of her skin. Maybe it was just plain nervousness. His fingers might as well have been toes.

"Here, let me do it." She reached behind her neck and in a moment she had fastened the clasp. "Got it. Sometimes these things are tricky. My fingers are used to it. I'm a girl."

She lowered her collar and opened a button to show him how it sat. The fine thread sparkled golden on her brown chest, except for a few links hidden in the cleavage.

"How does it look?"

His lips parted, but no words came out. His eyes said, *I approve*.

She opened two more buttons on her shirt to display the golden links on her brown chest more fully. The thin links of the chain hooked on a button and she used her fingers to free it with a tug, the tug momentarily lifting the delicate fabric of the shirt, revealing a shadow of—

"How does it look?" she said again.

He bit his lip. What was he supposed to say? *The nipple? It's perfect.*

Happy face.

7

Bryce and Jessica were the school's most radiant couple. All the popular people wanted to share in their light. As one half of the most favored pair, Bryce had little time for his old companions. Jessica not only stole him away from Andrea, but from his old group: Tipp, Tadd, and Muscle Teeth.

Tipp and Tadd, though nerds, were somewhat cool, but they were ninth graders and considered too young to hang out with seniors, and, well, Muscle Teeth was an ultra nerd.

"He's never done this with a girl before," Muscle Teeth said. "What a traitor. I feel so betrayed."

They accepted Poe, a ninth grader and a nerd, because Bryce insisted that they do.

When Poe hung out with Bryce and his new friends, cool as they were (yawn), he longed to be with Andrea. Claiming that he needed to study, he would often leave from "partying" with them (yawn) and go home. He would call her at 10:00 and they would talk until 2:00, their beloved 2:00.

He could listen to her voice all night. He could talk to her forever and feel neither hunger nor need for sleep. He could listen to the music in her voice forever.

8

Bryce inquired about her frequently, even when Jessica was sitting right next to him. What he really wanted to know was if she was going with anyone.

"Not yet," Poe said.

"That's good."

"Indeed," answered Poe mysteriously, "that is very good."

9

More and more, he was eating lunch with Andrea instead of with Bryce and his new group. He enjoyed these private lunches with Andrea. They talked on the phone all the time, but seeing her in real life was better. The sight of her wearing his chain was exhilarating. He imagined her in his arms. If they got married as soon as they graduated and lived to be eighty, that would be sixty-three years. Not enough. They would have to take good care of their health and live until ninety. That would be seventy-three years together. Was that enough? Could they live to be a hundred? And after that, could they be together in heaven?

"You have handsome ears," she said at lunch.

"They're mismatched."

"I think they're handsome. They make you handsome."

"Thank you."

"You have nice lips," she said.

He set his fork on the edge of the plate.

"I think it would be nice to kiss you," she said.

He wiped his mouth with the napkin.

"Well?" she said.

"Kiss who, *me?*"

"You, Poe. You."

His heart drummed a rapid tattoo in his chest. "I think it would be nice to kiss you too," he said.

"Kiss who, *me?*"

"You, Andrea. You."

"Hahaha."

"Tehehe."

She moved her face close to his. He was a statue.

"Kiss me," she said. "What's wrong?"

"I have to ask Bryce first."

Without a word, she picked up her tray and dumped her uneaten meatloaf in the trash bin.

For a second, he had thought she was going to dump it on his head.

10

That night, she wouldn't answer his calls, so he called Bryce.

"Do I have your permission to kiss Andrea?"

"Absolutely not."

"Okay," Poe said. "Good night."

"Good night," Bryce said.

11

Bryce called back three minutes later.

"Can I tell you why it's not okay to kiss her?"

"Bryce, if you say I can't kiss her, then I won't kiss her. My loyalty is with you."

"Cool. Good night."

"Good night, Bryce."

"And stop calling me Bryce."

Poe's voice spiraled to a screeching falsetto: "I've never had a girlfriend, you have Jessica, and Andrea is amazing, but if you say I can't have her, then I'll call you Bryce all I want!"

"Tehehe," Bryce laughed.

Poe hung up the phone.

12

Poe worried that Bryce wouldn't call.

He feared his behavior had ended their friendship.

As one hour became two, he considered calling him back to apologize for the rashness of his actions. Bryce was his best friend and greatest champion. Bryce's charisma righted his listing spirit. Bryce's love buoyed his soul.

Andrea made him feel good about himself. She made him feel safe from his dark dreams of viscera, of dead rats, of voices from the grave.

Bryce was his sun. Andrea was his moon.

He needed them both to exist.

13

The phone rang.

"Bryce."

"Don't call me Bryce."

"Gerardo."

"I said no because we are brothers, and brothers don't betray brothers."

"I really do like her, brother."

"Brothers don't betray brothers," Bryce said, and Poe allowed him a silent pause to consider what *betrayal* meant. Preventing a brother from experiencing love when you have so much that it spills over is a betrayal, and a selfish one too. "I'm jealous, Poe."

"You are selfish."

"I'm not."

"You have Jessica. You want Andrea too. You want it all."

"No, I am a . . ."

"A selfish cad."

"*Cad?* What is that?"

"Look it up."

Bryce inhaled deeply, then exhaled. "I don't know what it is about her, but I still like her. I know that I hurt her, and you won't. But I still want her, and I hate seeing her with anyone else, especially you."

"Especially me?" Poe said.

"She'll turn you against me. We've been friends since kindergarten. She's not even that cute. Do you see those braces? You would kiss that mouth, really?"

"Yes, I would kiss that mouth. Happily!" Bryce had never made Poe angry. He had always made Poe feel nothing but good, but now he was angry. "Do I have your blessings to accept her kiss, or not?"

In response, sniffing sounds came from the other end of the line. After a moment, Poe identified the sniffing as sobs. "You can do whatever you want, but please don't."

Poe let him have a good cry. He imagined Bryce curled up on the bed like he did back when they were kids during sleepovers. His dad wouldn't let him stay an extra night, and he cried, Bryce the tough guy.

When he spoke, his voice was puffy like eating a pillow: "This is embarrassing."

"It's okay to show your soft side to me, Bryce."

"What?!"

"Soft."

Bryce was silent, and then he said, "Poe, what I'm going to do next has nothing to do with you. It's about me."

"What are you going to do?"

"I'm going to hang up on you abruptly."

"Bryce, it's not abrupt if you take the time to explain it."

"Stop calling me Bryce!"

"Tehehe."

Bryce hung up.

14

At lunch the next day, they ate with their heads down, neither of them speaking, their plastic forks scraping the trays lightly. When Poe glanced up, he found her staring.

"Well?" she said.

Poe sipped the last of his milk from the carton and set it down. "We have his permission to kiss," he said.

"Permission!" She flung her bread at his face. "Bryce, Bryce, Bryce. I won't kiss you until you get out from under his spell."

So, there was no kiss that day. There was no kiss that week. There was no kiss that month. There was no kiss that year.

Welcome to the friend zone, brother.

III Handsome Men

Junior year, Poe and Andrea were everywhere together: at the movies, at the skating rink, at all of Bryce's games.

At homecoming, Poe blew her kisses from the bleachers as she marched with the band at halftime. She acknowledged him with a sweeping tilt of her flute and one step that was extra high. She wouldn't kiss him, but he kept trying.

—At the Thanksgiving Day Ball, he held her body close and they slow danced to their favorite song: "I'll Be Your Lover" by III Handsome Men.

She sang in his ear, "*I'll be your lover.*"

He sang back, "*Whenever, forever. Just say you want me to. Do you want me to?*"

She did not answer, but their bodies rubbed against each other, their loins burning.

—At the Christmas dance, he proposed marriage. She said yes.

"And where shall we make our home, my love?" he asked as they slow danced with their cheeks touching.

"Anywhere with you, my love."

"And how many children shall we have, my love?"

"As many as you wish, my love."

"I wish for a dozen, my love."

"For you, I would bear two dozen, my love."

"And what shall our first born be named?"

"Zoe if it's a girl."

"Zander if it's a boy."

"Hahaha."

"Tehehe."

He sang in her ear, "*Whenever, forever. Just say you want me to*. Do you want me to?"

She uttered no words, but squeezed his hand ever so slightly.

When the song ended, they strolled casually to the door, past cardboard Santa and his eight teenaged reindeer toting surfboards draped with tinsel and blinking Christmas lights, but outside where no one could see, the lovers dashed to her car, sped to her house, and sprinted up the stairs to her room.

—He held his breath as she stepped out of her dress. *This is it,* he thought.

Unfastening her bra, she turned away. Still shy, she refastened it.

He was shy too, but he drew near, and she allowed his arms to encircle her waist. He nuzzled her hair, her cheek, her neck. Her dancer's sweat, her body's secret odors—my God! He felt he would burst.

Downstairs, her half sisters listened to a carol on the CD player as they wrapped Christmas gifts beside the silver-and-blue menorah.

"Dashing through the snow, in a one-horse open sleigh."

He whispered into her skin: "Whenever, forever. Just say you want me to."

Her voice was low, husky. "I want you to," she said.

"Over fields we go, laughing all the way."

Her eyes were dreamy, her body trembling in his arms. He approached her lips the way Bryce had taught him. *Move halfway there. Stop. Put a finger gently under her chin.*

Wait for her to make up the distance. Let her kiss you.

He was executing it perfectly, but she grabbed his finger.

"That's his move, right? He taught you that."

"Why make such a fuss? It's just a kiss."

"*His* kiss."

When he made another attempt to kiss her, she put a palm over his mouth and pushed him away.

"*What fun it is to ride and sing a sleighing song tonight!*"

Delicious Christmas Cake

On Monday at lunch, they were served a square of Christmas cake with their chicken and mashed potatoes. The cake was chocolate with a choice of red or green frosting. Andrea chose red. Poe chose green.

She frosted her pinkie and passed it over his lips. He frosted his pinkie and passed it over hers. They counted to three and each licked the other's pinkie.

"You think?"

"Really now."

"Whatever."

There was no difference in taste between the red and the green. The taste, however, was a sweet beyond delicious. And the potential? Now they spoke with silent smiles and mischievous eyes.

What else might be tasted?

Lips, perhaps.

Mine, perhaps?

Yours most definitely, perhaps.

He moved his face to hers. She moved hers to his.

Bryce plunked down at their table, interrupting their silent discussion.

"What's up, old buddy?"

Moving his face away from Andrea's, Poe grunted in response.

"It's cool, man."

Suzy Arkanian, the latest beauty queen Bryce was dating, plunked down on the cafeteria's old-style bench seat and slid next to him and across from Andrea. She fluttered her well-manicured fingers in greeting, the nails painted red and green for the season. "Hey, guys."

Suzy Arkanian, who had kitten-like eyes and was perfumed like Christmas cinnamon, was an actual beauty queen, having worn a tiara and a sparkling taffeta gown as she was paraded down A1A through South Beach on a float in last year's Orange Bowl parade. Soft-voiced and blond, Suzy made Palmetto Cove Senior High proud as one of ten finalists for Miss Miami Teen USA. She finished second runner-up to a slim, graceful girl with brunette curls from a wealthy private school, but earned a full scholarship to the University of Miami.

Suzy was an honors student in the running for valedictorian when they graduated next year. Andrea, who would actually become next year's valedictorian, was Suzy's natural enemy. They were both smart and they had both dated Bryce. Suzy was gentle as a lamb but wise as a serpent, Andrea warned Poe.

Poe thought Suzy was okay, but Andrea did not permit him to like her. Andrea did not permit him to like any girl. Andrea only permitted him to like Andrea. He was all hers, and she would not share. She would not kiss him, but her jealousy was a sign he was getting close.

The conversation was dull, as it always was when someone, even Bryce, joined them. They couldn't say the sweet, clever things to each other when people were around, but Bryce had no problem showing his affection for the silent, cinnamon-smelling Suzy, whom Andrea hated. Suzy held Bryce's hand as he fed her red-frosted Christmas cake on a spoon. Suzy's conniving eyes remained on Andrea as her perfect teeth nibbled cake. The trip to their table had been a ruse. Suzy was here with Bryce to make Andrea jealous, yet Andrea was long over Bryce. Andrea had Poe now.

They spoke with their eyes.

You think?

Really now.

Whatever.

Last night, they had made up. Andrea had forgiven his Saturday-night faux pas. They had discussed their relationship. Where it was headed. How good it was, and it *was* good. She agreed to his seventy-three-year plan, and after death to be with him in heaven. As they talked, their song played in his room on a loop loud enough for her to hear it through the phone. *"Whenever, forever. Just say you want me to."* Over and over it played until she told him to turn it off.

"I get the message, but don't overdo it. Let's not have a repeat of Saturday night."

—When Bryce and Suzy got up to leave, Poe, mesmerized, rose with them.

Andrea cleared her throat. "Where are you going?"

Realizing what he had done, he quickly sat back down.

They watched as Bryce kissed Suzy, a gentle finger stroking her chin—the way he had taught Poe to kiss.

Andrea noted this, and when they left she glared at him. "Get out from under his spell. Don't answer his calls. Don't bring him up in our conversations. Cut him off for a week."

"I won't do it."

"*One week.*"

"I can't do it."

"Then no kiss."

"But you're my girlfriend."

"Oh yeah?" She got up and mashed what was left of her

red-frosted Christmas cake on his head. "Bryce is your girl-friend! Go ask Bryce for a kiss!"

—As children, they had invented scenarios that had them born as siblings in the same family. In the fantasy, Bryce's mother would be *their* mother, and sometimes Poe's mother would be *their* mother. Poe's father was always *their* father, and Bryce's father did not count.

He and Bryce were each other's brother. Staying away from his brother was too harsh a prohibition. No. He wouldn't do it. He wouldn't even try. Gerardo's parents had named him Gerardo, so Poe had gone to the dictionary and found a more suitable name for his brother. He had named him Bryce, "the freckled one." It frustrated Gerardo that Poe called him Bryce. Poe told him mysteriously, "You know why."

"But I don't have freckles."

"You're lying."

"I'm not lying."

"Pull down your pants. Let me see your pee-pee."

"What!"

When Bryce wouldn't play along, Poe would pull down his own pants and start shaking his ten-year-old, freckled pee-pee like a maraca.

Thing 2 and Thing 1

Poe's bedroom was spotless, of course, with only four pieces of furniture in it: a desk and chair for his schoolwork, a tall bookshelf that held his schoolbooks arranged by height, and his tidy bed with its lone pillow in a white pillowcase, which he fluffed once in the morning and again at night before he said his prayers. To avoid messing up the sheets, he almost never sat on his bed, only slept on it.

Andrea, whenever she came over, insisted that they sit on the bed. He would've preferred that she sit in the chair while he sat on the floor Indian-style looking up at her, worshipping her, or even better that they both sit on the floor, with their shoulders touching. But she insisted that they sit on the bed.

As they sat on his bed a week after the Christmas-cake incident, his mind kept going back to a recurring image he had of them lying on the bed together, faceup, holding hands, pondering the naked ceiling.

They exchanged gifts.

Her to him: a semi-expensive gold watch.

Him to her: Forever Yours, a perfume that boasted the fragrance and warmth of a fairy-tale fireplace. It came in a pink crystal bottle shaped like a heart, and at $16.98 was the most expensive perfume on the discount shelf at Walgreens.

Her to them both: matching T-shirts. *Thing 2 and Thing 1. Thing 1 and Thing 2.*

Him to them both: two tickets to see *Titanic.*

Wearing their matching T-shirts under Science Club sweaters, they entered the dark movie theater as the wounded ship began to sink on-screen. They were late, but had seen it before and would see it again, for it was their favorite movie.

Holding hands, they took their seats. She was more receptive than on the night of the faux pas. He nuzzled her neck. Her hair. Her skin. *This is it,* he thought.

When he came close to her lips, she said, "No."

Poe said, "No *what?*"

Andrea reminded, "No. '*Whenever, forever.*' No. '*Just say you want me to.*' No."

"Oh, *that* no," Poe said glumly.

"Yes. *That* no."

"Please."

"Stop begging."

On-screen the passengers of the unsinkable *Titanic* search for things that will float. Rose, who is from the upper deck, searches for Jack. There is a seat on a lifeboat reserved for her. She should be boarding a lifeboat with the other entitled aristocrats from the upper deck, but Jack who taught her to dance with abandon, Jack who taught her to spit like a man, Jack from the lower deck, Jack her true love, is missing. And Rose, frantically searching, will not take her seat on the lifeboat until she has found him. It was Andrea and Poe's favorite scene.

"Kiss me, Andrea. I mean it."

"Not gonna do it."

"Do you even like me?"

"I like you."

"This relationship is so immature."

"That's the way I like it," Andrea said, "for now."

"Yeah. Okay," Poe said, and sulking, he faced the screen and sank like an anchor into his seat.

On-screen Rose finds Jack in a holding cell, his hands chained together around an iron pipe. There is an axe on the wall. She has never swung an axe before, but she takes it down. Jack's eyes grow large. If the axe lands imperfectly—whack. Severed fingers or worse, a severed hand. Then he studies her face. The ship is sinking and she is here with him. She could've saved herself. She would rather die with him than live without him. This is *his* Rose. He trusts her. He inhales a hard breath, giving her the signal, and with one desperate swing and a chop that miraculously hits its mark, Rose frees him from the chains. Then they kiss.

Andrea turned to Poe. "If you had kissed me that first day, it would've been okay, but my feelings for you have changed. It's more serious now. If I kiss you, I'm afraid of what might happen."

"You kissed Bryce."

"He was a gentleman."

"And?"

"I didn't like him as much."

Poe sat up slowly. "So . . ."

Andrea placed a hand on either side of his face. "Yes. I'm a virgin," she said.

A virgin.

Aha, that explained it. She liked him, but she was a virgin. He had been pressuring a virgin. What a shame. And what about *his* secret? It should've been obvious. When would he have lost it, and with whom? Sometimes the obvious needed to be said. He studied her face. He trusted her. He said, "I'm a virgin too."

"What?! Hahaha."

"Tehehe."

"Hahaha."

Now they both understood, and the pressure was off. She

would no longer feel the pressure to yield. He would no longer feel the pressure to demand. He would no longer have to make attempts at it as a rite of passage into that brotherhood of high school boyfriends with girlfriends. He could simply love her with no pressure. It may not be normal, but it was okay with him.

Someone behind them told them to shut up.

"You think?" Andrea whispered.

"Really now," Poe whispered back.

"Whatever," Andrea said, and her lips were on his.

Peck.

—After the peck, she sat back.

In the flickering lights of the theater, her face came into full view and her smile melted into teenage-girl seriousness. She removed her peppermint gum and stuck it to the back of her hand. She held his face in her hands and brought him to her slowly until their lips touched. Their teeth clacked, their noses tried to fit, this was his first kiss, she had some experience, though not much, but their need to have each other was strong and somehow their tongues met in that happy chaos of the senses.

He had finally gotten it, but now it was not even about getting it. He loved her. He loved her. He loved her, and she loved him.

It Matters to Me

The last day of classes before Christmas break, Poe stared at himself in the mirror.

Uncombed hair. A pale face spotted with freckles and peach fuzz. Oversized clothes floating on a flabby frame.

He went to his closet. This year's wardrobe was mostly Science Club T-shirts and jeans. For church, he had two over-sized blue shirts and a pair of fat-boy pants.

Shoes? One pair of no-name sneakers and a pair of tight-fitting penny loafers inherited from his father.

"This will not do," he had told Bryce yesterday after the incident. "They laugh at her because she's with me. I'm an embarrassment to her."

Bryce had assured him, "Andrea's not like that. It doesn't matter to her."

It was true. But yesterday when he and Andrea walked arm in arm to class, Jefferson and Chucho, two obnoxious boys who had made his life miserable since middle school, said loudly, "Such a cute couple," and broke into laughing so uncontrollably they coughed.

They had done this before, but yesterday Andrea had had enough. She let go of Poe's hand and walked to the other side of the hall where the obnoxious pair posed before their open lockers. What did they keep in their lockers? They were never seen with any books. Jefferson took out a brownish bottle of mouthwash. Chucho took out a folded paper bag, which he tucked under his arm. He was the school weed man. This was where he stashed his weed. Poe couldn't make out clearly most of what Andrea said to them, but Jefferson and Chucho accepted it patiently, their faces silent and mock serious.

On her way back to Poe, she threw the final words over her shoulder to his tormentors: "Yes, that's right, we *are* cute. But you're a cute couple too."

"Oh shit!" Chucho said, and slapped Jefferson five.

Jefferson spit mouthwash on the ground and said, "Andrea is a badass."

They went down the hall shaking with laughter. Between their peals of laughter a word floated back to him: "Obese."

"What did they say?"

Andrea took Poe's hand. "Ignore them. They're just jealous. What they say doesn't matter."

—"It matters to me," Poe said to his reflection in the mirror as he dressed for school. "This has got to change."

He chose the Science Club T-shirt with the fewest wrinkles and his best pair of jeans. He took two steps out the door, then turned around.

He stood before the mirror again. He looked like he had just stepped out of a drier. Lumpy. Wrinkled.

He pulled off his *I ♥ Science* T-shirt, set it on the ironing board, and bulldozed the wrinkles with the steaming iron. Then he pulled off his fat-boy jeans and set them on the ironing board. He took his time with the iron. He did the best he could. One more look in the mirror. Wrinkle-free, sure, but there were other things wrong. He appeared haphazardly put together. There was an imbalance, an unevenness of framing. Like soup in a sack—chunks of him sloshed too much to one side of the frame. No matter how he posed, no matter how he sucked in his stomach and pushed out his chest, he couldn't bring it back into the frame. He closed his eyes and wished the ugly away, but when he opened them, Mr. Soup in a Sack was still there.

He hated Jefferson and Chucho like he never had before. He spent fifteen minutes debating whether to go to school or stay home, but he had to see Andrea. He had to show her she was right, that their words didn't matter, though they did.

He arrived to school late, feeling uncomfortable in his own skin. As he and Andrea ate lunch that day at their table in the school cafeteria, Jefferson and Chucho cracked jokes at their table with the other bad characters at Palmetto Cove Senior High, a long-limbed, mostly male group, notorious for their disruptive behavior, harsh hairstyles, and cool (odd) fashion choices. The jokes at that cool (odd) table were loud and vicious. They kept saying that word, the one fancy word they knew. *Obese*. But they weren't targeting him. The janitor, Mr. Henry, was a soft-voiced brown man, the nicest adult at the school. He had a large behind. He was obese too. The jokes were about poor Mr. Henry and his janitorial crew taking down the Christmas decorations—a crew that Jefferson and Chucho would no doubt be working on a few Christmases from now if they weren't in prison or in their graves.

Poe smiled and said, "In their graves."

Andrea touched his hand. "Who? Oh yeah. Them. Ignore them. They're stupid."

"You think?"

"Really now."

"Whatever," he said, and they laughed.

But thinking about them in their graves had made his penis hard. He thought it only worked with rats.

—He started cutting his hair regularly and got a part-time job delivering pizzas so he could shop for clothes at the better stores in the mall.

He joined Gym Club and started lifting weights. He had shot up in height since ninth grade and now at 6'2" was a head taller than most. By the end of junior year, Poe had lost fifty soft pounds, and gained it back as sculpted muscle. Poe's body had transformed to the point where the football coach stopped him in the hall and tapped the *I* ♥ *Science* logo on his Science Club T-shirt. "Science Club? What are you, 6'2", 230, 240? You're big enough to play middle linebacker in the NFL. You should be on the football team."

Poe didn't like sports.

He wanted to look good for Andrea, who was beautiful. He wanted to be a man she was proud to be seen with. He was so in love, he lived for her eyes only.

Unbeknownst to him, he was living for someone else's eyes too.

THE GHOUL

Stupid Mary

It was the second day of the second week of senior year. The game was called "Stupid Mary," and it was popular among the nerds of the Science Club. Neither Andrea nor Poe started it, but they were the most enthusiastic of its players. They played it that day after a two-minute make-out session at his locker. Muscle Teeth was there too, for it required at least three to play.

"She is stupid," said Andrea.

"Stupid?" asked Poe.

"Impressively stupid," said Muscle Teeth.

"Are you saying that Mary Fisk is stupid?" asked Poe. Poe was the best straight man.

"Unabashedly stupid," said Andrea, who was the best with adverbs.

"Oppressively stupid," added Muscle Teeth, who was good with adverbs too, though not as good as Andrea, who had observed Mary speaking too long with Poe in Science Club that day. Poe was hers and hers alone.

"But is she stupid?" Poe asked.

"Profoundly stupid."

"Irretrievably stupid."

"Undeniably stupid."

"But is Mary Fisk stupid?"

They heard a sniffle and turned.

How long had Mary Eugenia Fisk, the ghoul, been standing there? She stood awash in tears waiting for one of them to apologize or say they were just kidding around. When none of the others opened their mouths, Poe turned to her and opened his: "Mary, we didn't mean anything by it."

He took a step in her direction, but Andrea hooked his arm, holding him back, and he abruptly closed his mouth.

Mary Eugenia Fisk, the ghoul, walked away, both hands pushing tears from her face, and the game started up again.

"Unwittingly stupid."

"Inarticulately stupid."

"Incomprehensibly stupid."

This time the target was Suzy Arkanian, but there was no straight man as Poe refused to play his part.

2

On Wednesday, he found a note on his desk: *I know you didn't meen anything by it.*

The note was from the ghoul. He showed it to Andrea, who had a good laugh.

"She can't even spell the word *mean*."

—On Thursday, he found another note: *You were like forced to do it. It was like pear pressure, right?*

Andrea had a good laugh over that one too.

"She doesn't know the difference between *pear* and *peer*."

—On Friday, he got another note: *I like you.*

He didn't show this note to Andrea. He didn't believe Andrea would laugh if he showed her this note.

He pondered the note all evening while he and Andrea talked until their beloved 2:00. Then he pondered it all weekend.

—On Monday, he got another note: *Did you get my last note? If so, teer it up. You are a snob just like the rest of them.*

This note perplexed him.

What had he done between notes to make her stop liking him?

—For the rest of the week, he watched her.

He watched her in Science Club, spouting scientific nonsense to the nerds, but winning the argument with a far more convincing theorem. Her beauty. Though they regarded her mediocre knowledge with laughing disdain, they could not help but succumb to her matchless weapons of the flesh. Her perfectly formed face. Her beguiling eyes. A chance touch when she brushed past could make them giddy.

The cool nerds Tipp and Tadd were particularly smitten.

Tipp said, "Today she grazed my neck. Dare I dream it— she loves me. I swoon. I shall never wash this neck again."

Tadd said, "Please wash your neck, you dweeb. Your smell is foul enough already to sicken. On the other hand, she does seem to have amped it up a notch. I wonder what happened. Have you any thoughts, Poe?"

"None at all," he said, but wondered if it had something to do with the notes.

—He watched her between classes in conversations with her friends. On Thursday, he heard her say, "Poe," or so he believed. It floated to him on gossamer wings, the whispered song of a sweetly singing bird.

Was the conversation about him?

—He hid in the back of the auditorium where it was dark as she practiced scales with the school chorus, her mellow contralto voice the music of a pleasant dream.

She turned her face to where he sat.

He ducked down between the seats.

—On Friday, he walked past the courts during tennis team practice, but she was not there. He wanted to watch her practice. He wanted to watch her swing the racket and hit the balls.

He wanted her to explain the notes.

She emerged from the locker room in a crowd of her friends.

The others were dressed for class in blue tops and jeans. Her top was the bright yellow of the Palmetto Cove Senior High School mascot—a blue and yellow bumblebee named Buzzer. Her tanned legs were exposed in shorts of school color blue. She shone among her friends.

She saw him and waved. He blushed, and quickly walked away.

—On Monday, he found another note: *Try harder.*

—He showed the note to Bryce and asked what he should do.

Bryce said, "She's one of those people, you know? She's *that* kind."

"Really?"

"She was fun, but I couldn't handle her."

"Is that why you guys broke up?"

"She was too pretty. Too many guys hit on her," he said. "And what are you gonna do about Andrea?"

"Andrea and I are fine."

"Yeah?"

"Yeah!" Poe said too forcefully.

Bryce grinned. *"Mary, Mary got him hooked,"* he sang to the tune of "Mary, Mary" by Run-DMC.

Poe scoffed. He tore the note into tiny pieces and sprinkled them in four trash cans.

3

"Nice car," said the ghoul about his mother's ten-year-old Buick.

It was Thursday two weeks later, a warm September day. There was something in the air. Everyone was coming down with the flu. Andrea had been out since Monday.

The ghoul leaned her head inside the window, her eyebrows stiff with mascara and her lips painted red. This was not a tennis-practice face, yet she had her racket and was dressed in a tennis team T-shirt and the short tennis team skirt. The painted lips said, "Can you give me a ride?"

Before he could respond, she had climbed in and sat down in the passenger seat, the scent of flowers following her in. "I live just down the road," she said, and began fiddling with the radio.

He made a face. "It doesn't work."

"It's one of those old-fashioned ones anyway." She lifted her hand from the broken radio. Her fingers were long, thin, and well-manicured, the nails painted bronze to match her hair. "Are you ever planning to get it fixed?"

"Next paycheck."

"Well, I'm not riding with you again until you get it fixed." She was kidding, right? Then again, there was that note. *I like you.*

He wanted her out of the car. What if someone saw? He turned the key in the ignition until a grating sound reminded that the car was already started.

She pulled the seat belt over her shoulder, and the form of her slim, athletic bosoms danced in the fabric of her white tennis shirt. She clicked the seat belt and observed, "You know, with a car so roomy you can have adventures and your parents would never know a thing. Is Andrea adventurous? Anyway, she's lucky to have a boyfriend with a car."

"Andrea has her own car. A BMW." He glanced in his rearview mirror. Students in yellow and blue milled about casually. No one seemed to be paying any attention to them.

"Her little BMW is much too small for adventures," the ghoul said. She tugged at her seat belt, trying to get comfortable. "Your car is strong. I like a strong buck. Sorry, I meant *Buick*."

He had to ignore her. But that note.

I like you.

He glanced in the mirror again. All clear. He tapped the gas, and the Buick slowly backed out of the parking space. He turned the wheel and it rolled through the parking lot filled with students and out onto the road facing east.

"This way?"

"Yeah." She had stopped tugging at her seat belt and was comfortable now. She set the racket in her lap and settled back in her seat. She waited a few moments and then touched a hand to his large biceps. "You must work out a lot."

A smile appeared briefly on his face. Yes, he worked out. He had gone from a chubby, pretend nerd to a well-built gym rat. His body must be stronger and prettier for Andrea when she decided they should move beyond kissing.

He had gotten a peek at her emerging from the shower on Saturday, her bathrobe hanging casually open—the curving, dizzying path of unblemished honey-brown skin from her hips to her face, a path of forbidden crevices and ample body parts still dotted with water from the shower. The robe quickly flapped closed and she ordered him out of the room while she dressed, as though they hadn't been making out on her bed fifteen minutes earlier.

Smart, Andrea, smart.

The delightful image was burned into his brain as a covenant. *All of me will be yours if you behave yourself.* The covenant made him steel. No temptation could break him. But as he drove east on 49th Street in silence, he wondered at the ghoul's hair.

Her twin ponytails were burnished bronze while the skin of her arms was dusted with fine golden hairs. Was she bronze? Was she gold? What prize was she?

The note had said, *I like you.* What did it mean?

He went to speak, and she slapped his face.

"Stop looking at my legs, pervert!"

4

She slapped him again. "Let me out! I'll walk."

"But I wasn't looking."

"Yes you were!"

She raised her hand to slap again, and he caught her arm. It was slender like a spring twig in his hand. A sudden flinch and it would break. His face stung like on the citrus ride in Tampa. He hadn't been looking at her legs, though he had been *planning* to look. He had planned to have his pleasure cautiously, for she had a body he admired. Now that Andrea was sick, he had been following the ghoul more aggressively. He had watched her at tennis practice today. At tennis practice, there was no lipstick and mascara. Now there was lipstick and mascara. Were the lipstick and mascara for him? He released her hand, and she sat in silence, except for the sound of her breathing.

He opened his mouth to apologize, and she shut it with a finger.

"Look all you want. That's what legs are for."

He stepped on the gas and the Buick shot ahead.

5

They crossed a small bridge. Forty-ninth Street became 103rd, Hialeah became Palmetto Cove, and the ghoul said: "Turn here."

He turned onto a street where the sunlight came filtered through a dense canopy of leaves. The enormous banyan trees, their branches long overdue for pruning, cast a shadowy gloom over the area. They were in Pickett Park, an older section of Palmetto Cove known for its neglected appearance and its scruffy-looking, demoralized residents.

"That's my house over there."

She pointed to a double-wide trailer with blue-striped awnings, a tin can on cement blocks in the middle of other tin cans on cement blocks, their lawns poorly maintained and dotted with small purple flowers.

Pickett Park was named after George Pickett, the Confederate general who gave his name to the courageous but unsuccessful counterattack on the last day of the Battle of Gettysburg: Pickett's Charge. In this blighted neighborhood that bore his name, there was not a white picket fence in sight. Old people and the poor lived in the trailers. Down the street from the ghoul's home loomed the Pickett Park housing projects whose walls were so heavily covered in gang markings and graffiti that scarce little of the original redbrick façade remained. Mostly brown people lived there. Around the corner was the Palmetto Cove Municipal Solid Waste Transfer Site, a towering landfill that everyone called Mt. Trash-More.

They used chemicals to mask the smell, but late at night when the sun was gone, the odor was unbearable. As children, they were warned to be on their guard when passing through this neighborhood. Sadness, crime, and a foul smell lived here.

He parked, but left the engine running.

"Would you like to come in?"

"No."

"My parents aren't home," she told him. He said no again, with his eyes. She ignored his eyes and continued casually talking: "One of my sisters might be here, but she won't bother us. Judy. You'll like her, she's pretty. It seems beauty comes in fives. Cindy, Judy, Dixie, and Dottie. I'm the baby. They're all grown with families of their own. Sometimes they leave and come back home for a while. You know how it is."

"I don't know how it is."

"They break up and then get back together." She shook her head as though he should already know this. "They live with their boyfriends—sometimes—but that's not going to be me. I'm better than that." She was the best on the team, with a national ranking and scholarship offers. "I'm going to make it out," she said, tapping the tennis racket, "with this." Poe watched her face in profile. In Tampa, she had worn her hair upswept with fluttering bangs. Today, twin ponytails bound together with black ribbon hung down to the middle of her back. "Come inside, there's something I want you to see."

"I can't." Her hand was on his biceps again. "I've got to go see Andrea. She is not well."

"You're a faith healer?"

"Eh?"

She squeezed his biceps and nodded approvingly. "If you're not a faith healer, she doesn't need you. You'll get sick yourself hanging around her. Now, if you were a doctor, maybe. Are you a doctor?"

"Eh?"

"You're not a doctor either. What you are is a good boy-friend. I wish I had a boyfriend like you. So loyal," she said. "Come inside. I want to show you something. Don't worry, I'm not going to throw you down and kiss you."

"Eh?"

She was called the ghoul because in fourth grade it was said she had kissed her best friend Tina. Everyone knew the rumor. He had always wondered if it were true.

"Turn off the engine."

"No."

"Turn it off."

He turned off the engine.

"Are you asking for a kiss?" she said.

"What? No."

"Because if you're asking, let me be honest, I'm not sure what to say. You are cute, and I do like you."

"I did not ask."

"Yes you did. You inferred it by turning off the engine."

"Not *infer*," he corrected. "The word you mean is *imply*."

He was not trying to be mean, but quick as that, her mood changed.

"Oh, Poe, you're a snob just like Andrea."

"No. No. I'm not a snob."

"You don't think I'm smart."

"I do think you're smart."

"You're not telling the truth," she said, pouting.

"Yes, I am telling the truth," he lied, and he didn't know why he lied, as her hand moved slowly over his skin.

"You're lying to be nice."

"I'm not lying," he lied, to be nice.

"Liar."

Outside the Buick, two boys tossed a football back and

forth. They were shirtless, their bare chests marked up with brash tattoos. Jefferson and Chucho. In middle school, Jefferson had slapped him on the back of the head. No warning. Just walked up and slapped the back of his head. "Fat-ass bitch," Jefferson had said. His partner in crime, Chucho, had laughed. Bullies. They deserved to live in Pickett Park. They were *that* kind of people.

The ghoul brought her face close to his. That scent. Those flowers. It was some kind of face cream, some kind of perfume. Her overly red lipstick perhaps. No, her lipstick smelled like crayon. "Hey, liar," her crayon-red lips said, "look at me."

He found himself lost in the blue-gray sea of her eyes. The ghoul lifted the racket from her lap and set it on the floor in preparation to make out.

She leaned in. He leaned back. He was steel and wouldn't break. She found his resistance amusing. "Poor little Poe. Such nice lips, and Andrea is too contagious to kiss you."

"I can wait."

"Andrea owns you."

"No she doesn't."

"Black girls are notoriously possessive," she said. "Unabashedly possessive, unapologetically possessive."

"She doesn't own me."

He was steel, and he reached for the key in the ignition.

"Don't touch that. We're just talking. I like talking to you, Poe, that's all."

He lifted his hand from the key. He wasn't sure where to put it. She pulled it onto her lap where it was warm, but he was steel. Her tennis skirt was school color blue and short. She made a slight movement and her skirt shifted, revealing more tanned thigh. Steel snapped like plywood.

She made a face. "There's something you're not telling

me. You're a virgin, right?" When he lowered his head, she put her hand atop his in her lap. "But it's okay."

"We're not virgins."

"*We?* Andrea too? She's not only a snob, she's a frigid one too!" The ghoul put her face against his cheek and laughed into his skin. It was loud, shaking, unembarrassed laughter, which dampened the peach-fuzz skin near his nose. The dampness smelled like mint. When he opened his mouth to speak, she silenced him with a kiss.

"Your lips are soft," she said when it ended.

Her lips were soft too. Her skin was golden, and warm, and her hair was bronze, or golden, and her perfume was the scent of purple flowers, wilted flowers in the rain. His father was buried in the rain.

His father was stabbed by his cellmate and bled out on the floor. He wasn't found until first check the next day. The prison gave them the body, but Poe's mother gave it back. She couldn't afford to bury him.

"Kiss me," said the ghoul.

He kissed her, and she tasted like rain. Her hand moved from his biceps to his pants. She tasted like rain, prison-grave-yard rain. He loved his father. Poe and his mother attended the funeral in the prison graveyard while it rained.

Her hand in his lap unzipped him. He pushed her hand away.

"Don't fight it, virgin. Kiss with tongue."

He kissed with tongue.

She gagged. "Too much tongue."

They kissed again, correctly this time.

—The two boys across the street who had been tossing the football earlier were leaned up against a dying coconut tree watching. They were more interested in the action taking place in the Buick. Jefferson McBride was a dark-skinned Bahamian boy with a gap-tooth smile. The other boy's name was Pablo Rodriguez-Martinez, but everyone called him Chucho. Last week in the weight room Poe had bench-pressed 370 with ease. Chucho, who had been one of the three boys spotting him, was impressed. "Man, you're ripped. You're a monster. Why you don't play ball?" he had said. Watching him now, Chucho must have been impressed again.

The ghoul lifted her tennis shirt, folded the blue and yellow bumblebee emblem into the bunched-up material. One glance at the whiteness of her young girl's chest, and he closed his eyes. His fingers traced the skin of her breasts from memory.

"Use your lips, virgin."

His lips brushed the bare skin, which was warm and slick with perspiration. His tongue glided over the skin. It smelled like flowers. It tasted like rain. After the funeral, he had climbed the thick trunk of the live oak in their backyard up to the tree house he and Dada had built. He loved his dada and went up there to cry, but it was springtime and raining, and his mother called him inside.

He lifted his face from the ghoul's sweet-smelling flesh. "Andrea will know."

"Shhh. It'll be our secret." The ghoul pulled her tennis shirt back down over her nipples. "Come into the house. I have more things to show you."

Across the street, Chucho moved the football to the crook of his arm and applauded, then he tossed it to Jefferson, who grinned.

The ghoul exited the car first. Poe lagged behind enjoying the vision. She took off her shoes and walked on the ragged lawn. She picked a periwinkle from the lawn and tucked it behind her ear, and it was handsome there. She was indeed a vision, an enchantress, a goddess—much more than a beautiful barefoot girl with a periwinkle tucked behind her ear. Poe followed her into the house, and ten minutes later the mascara, the lipstick, and the periwinkle were the only things that remained after she had disrobed.

You Can't Have Her

There is a girl.

And her name is Andrea.

Andrea is smarter than the ghoul, so she considers her no threat. She even thinks of the ghoul as a friend, because the ghoul is too stupid to hold a grudge and Andrea condescends. When the ghoul says something outrageously nonscientific in Science Club, Andrea makes eye contact with you.

You think?

Really now.

Whatever.

Later over the phone, you agree with Andrea that the ghoul is oblivious to her own ignorance, as the ghoul waits for you in the double-wide trailer in Pickett Park, with a yard overgrown with weeds and periwinkles, and parents, a single mother and her unemployed boyfriend Roy, who are never at home. Where are they? Where are they, really? You've met each of her sisters, a listless, brunette-haired, doll-like quartet—Cindy, Judy, Dixie, and Dottie (who on occasion has asked to join you in bed with her sister). You've met all of their underdressed and poorly washed children: Robby, Mike, Joey, Fred, Ella Jean, Mike Jr., Elroy, Finny, John Paul, Angela, Bradley, Tommy, Phil, Christopher, Brittany, and Serena and Neeka the brown ones. You've met their sometimes jobless but consistently abusive boyfriends, one of whom used to slip into the ghoul's bedroom at night and fondle her until she started sleeping with a knife under her pillow.

"He got the message. I was only twelve, but I'm not going to take that from anybody," the ghoul proudly told you.

You've been to this place, this crowded trailer, a dozen times and seen her parents only once.

On their way out.

They are out now, and on this night you will engage in an illicit adventure with the ghoul until 9:30 p.m., after which you will return home and converse with Andrea over the phone from 10:00 p.m. until 1:15 a.m., for you cannot make it to 2:00, you cannot make it to 2:00, you try, but you're too sleepy and you cannot make it to your beloved 2:00.

Again.

Then, exhausted from the spirited conversation with one of your girls and the physically draining adventure with the other, you will go to sleep with Andrea on your mind and the taste of the ghoul on your lips.

You will dream of how good it felt to cuddle with the ghoul after the dirty deed was done tonight. How good it felt to hold her and talk of small things. The tennis scholarship she had been offered, your dream of going to culinary school after college and becoming a world-class chef, her crazy family, your dead father, her exes, your girlfriend. No topic was off-limits. She's had thirteen boyfriends, gone all the way with three: two seniors when she was a sophomore, a grown man last year, and no, he wasn't a teacher, and no, she won't tell you his name because it might get him in trouble, and then there was you. You were the fourth guy she went all the way with. You were the best by far. Yes, she went all the way with Tina. No, she didn't go all the way with Bryce.

"I wanted to. He didn't. He was a real gentleman."

No, the ghoul didn't actually hate Andrea. Andrea, she felt, had self-confidence issues due to her appearance. She was an ugly duckling. She was half black and she wore braces.

You disagreed. Andrea, you told her, was just fine with her looks, and she was gorgeous. She was no ugly duckling, a name you had warned the ghoul not to call her. No, no. The ghoul accused you of not understanding girls. She suggested a makeup tip you might mention to Andrea, a cream that would make her skin glow. It would work magic on her complexion, the ghoul assured. In your dream you see yourself telling Andrea about this cream that would make her skin glow, and what a surprise—she loves it. And loves you more for telling her about it. And loves the ghoul for telling you to tell her about it.

You wake up with a sharp intake of breath.

You cannot give Andrea this tip. If you gave Andrea this tip, she would kill you!

The ghoul is always doing sneaky things like this while cuddling. Cuddling with the ghoul is a bad thing. Cuddling is the bad thing you will miss the most when you break it off with her, because this bad thing, this cuddling, is so good.

—It is not good when a bad thing is good, and you like it so much that you'll sneak behind your girlfriend's back again, and again, and again, until not so long later, in the month of February, the shortest month of the year, when Valentine's Day falls on Saturday and the school celebrates it on the Friday before, you hand your girlfriend a mediocre Valentine's Day card: *I love you more than you will ever know.* You embrace her by the lockers as other students pass by, many of the girls clutching long-stemmed roses or hugging full bouquets to their breasts. You kiss your Andrea with the pain of regret, and she misreads your pain as passion.

"That was the best kiss ever, right?" she says, and you notice something is different about her. She opens her mouth.

"Your braces?"

"Gone. I got them out yesterday."

The next thing you know, you've ditched school, you're at her house, in her room, and she shuts the door and models for you as she walks to the bed, taking her time with each piece of clothing that she removes: her shirt, her jeans, her pink, lacy, heart-themed bra, her panties with the winged cupid, one pink arrow slotted in his bow.

Hands on her hips, she poses. "Take a picture," she says, "with your eyes."

You manage a weak smile and tepid applause.

Now she is on the bed, patting the mattress, waiting. When you stand there too long without undressing, she gets up from the bed and undresses you.

"You are beautiful," she says, admiring your body as your clothes are peeled away. That's when you realize that she is naked and you haven't complimented her.

"You too," you say, and follow her to the bed thinking, *I will tell her we can't do this, then run!*

You weren't able to meet with the ghoul last night and your treacherous body is shamelessly aroused. You hate yourself as you fall into Andrea's waiting arms.

She's older now with more flesh on her bones, and all of that marching to the drummer's beat has made the flesh on her bones taut, and you've experimented with her in this room in this big house with her grandmother's award-winning photographic portraits on the wall, arranged from large to small, but just enough of an imbalance, favoring the right side, an almost perfect golden ratio, which you've been tempted to adjust, only slightly adjust to make it perfect like Andrea's face, the perfect golden ratio, the divine proportion—it needs no adjusting—her face is beautiful, she is beautiful, and you've gone almost all the way, and now you *are* all the way, and she wants to kiss you as you do it, but you bite your lips as you turn from hers.

After it is over, you get up and begin putting back on your clothes.

She says, "Well, we finally did it."

You zip your jeans.

She says timidly, "I think it was good, don't you?"

You pull your T-shirt over your head, slide into it, and mumble a yes.

The day is chilly for mid-February in Miami. As you step into your sneakers, she covers up, but not from the cold. "You also didn't officially ask me to the prom. We're going, right?"

The prom. You forgot about the prom. You forgot about a lot of things. Grades. Responding to college acceptance letters. Saying *You're beautiful* to your beautiful girlfriend, who gave her love to you. How does prom matter now?

She is naked on the bed with the sheets held up to her breasts, covering them. She is confused, this girl who gave her virginity to you. "Did I do something wrong? Say something."

What are you supposed to say to that? How do you answer that?

You walk out of her room without a word. Outside the room, you pick up speed. As you rapidly descend the stairs, you hear her call your name.

"Poe."

It is then that you remember the final thing you forgot.

You forgot the best part.

You forgot to cuddle.

6

Bryce, Bryce, Bryce, if only you could call Bryce.

You are not sure how Bryce feels about you anymore. A rift has come between you and your best friend. He does not approve of your sneaking behind Andrea's back with Mary. You never thought such a thing could happen, that you treasure her cuddles more than you value his friendship. *Best friend* is such a childish concept. He used to hang out with you, now he hangs out with Muscle Teeth. You pass him in the halls and you barely speak, just head nods to acknowledge each other's existence. You haven't called him in two months. You miss his companionship, but there is Mary and her cuddling, and he's such a hypocrite. He had the nerve to tell you: "Don't do this to Andrea. It's not right."

"You should talk. How many girls are you dating now?" you said.

The master of disloyalty to girls gave a sly smile. "Two." Ashanti the brown cheerleader, and Judy the freshman, the porcelain Asian doll. "But they're not Andrea," he said.

"It's the same thing."

"No it's not," Bryce, the hypocrite, said.

This was in the hall outside the science classroom and Chucho the weed man walked past. Chucho, *your* weed man. You hang with Chucho and Jefferson now. They are uninteresting, and not really your friends, but they provide a service, so you tolerate their dullness. Chucho nodded and tapped the brown paper bag he kept the weed in.

You nodded back.

Bryce said, "You've changed, Poe."

"Change is good, right?"

Bryce said, "I've changed too." He hesitated before adding: "I'm in love this time."

"With who? Ashanti or the Chinese girl?"

"Neither. It's someone else."

You shook your head. "What? A third girl? Bro, you're way worse than me, so don't go all crazy with what I'm doing with Andrea and Mary."

Bryce said nothing. He opened the door to science class and went inside. You had science too, but Chucho, your weed man, was waiting for you in the boys' room. After Chucho, you skipped school and went to Mary's double-wide trailer to fuck.

Bryce, Bryce, Bryce, if only you could call Bryce. You wish you could talk to your best friend.

7

That night she phones.

"What's wrong? What did I do?"

"Nothing."

"Are we okay?"

"I don't know."

"Tell me."

"There's nothing to tell."

"Oh, you make me so mad."

"Andrea—"

She hangs up on you.

8

Seconds later she calls back.

You can hear it in her voice. She blames herself. Was she too boring, too smart, too stupid, too self-aware, too self-unaware, too much of a nerd? She has broken whatever it is you had and doesn't want to ruin it completely.

"If you would only tell me what I've done, I'm sure I can fix it. Whatever it is, I'm sorry. I won't do it again."

"It's my fault."

"What is your fault? *What?*"

"Andrea, I gotta go."

"Poe!"

Now it is you who hang up.

9

The phone rings again.

You pick up and her father says, "I just want you to know that you are like a part of the family, and families work together to get through things."

Now you are sobbing.

"It's okay, son," her father says.

He calls you *son*. Someone else's father calls you son. It's too much. This man, he's too good for you, this brown man who dared love a white woman. He possesses a courage you never will. Andrea has told you his story. A civil rights warrior attending Oberlin meets a Jewish woman with the same core values, the same beliefs, the same mission. Freedom from poverty and equality for all.

He majored in sociology. She was prelaw. They were both amateur musicians: he the jazz trumpeter; she the classical violinist. They were both born in December 1947: he the seventh, she the eighth. They seemed fated to meet and fall in love. She was spirited and soft-eyed. He was tall, dark, and silent except when talking about her. He could go on for hours singing her praises.

They were both in Selma in '65 with Dr. King. They cried in each other's arms in '68 when he died. Inseparable. Everyone loved them at Oberlin—not so much after they graduated and moved back to Alabama where he was born. He followed his heart and asked her to marry him. Why not? They were progressive. They had been living together since junior year at Oberlin.

It was 1972. Things needed to change, he thought. The racists didn't think so. The young couple suffered through flattened tires, public hostility, hate mail, and anonymous phone calls filled with anger and death threats. At the school where she taught English and directed the school choir and he taught social studies and directed the jazz band, they were shunned by colleagues white and black alike. As social justice warriors, they had expected this treatment. Fighting against it, they hoped to change the world, at least their little corner of it in Alabama. If this is what it took for change to come, then they would endure. They must set examples for their students, the hope for the future. Their students got it. Their students loved them.

She had always been sickly. Throughout the seventies, there were four miscarriages.

In 1982, when she found herself pregnant again, they moved back to her home state of Florida. Instead of a miscarriage this time, she had a successful childbirth. She held Andrea in her arms until she died.

This man—he overcame greater obstacles than you face now. Racism. Hate. The death of his true love. Your heart was for his daughter and it still is. Admit your crime before it's too late.

But you cannot. You take what you believe is the less difficult path.

"I gotta go, Mr. Stewart."

"Poe."

"I gotta go."

Courage like his, you do not possess.

10

Finally, you call Bryce.

"So, we're talking again?"

"I never said we weren't."

"Could have fooled me," he says. "So what's up?"

"Mary's pregnant."

He does not seem surprised. "You told Andrea yet?"

"I can't. How do you tell her something like that?"

"I see what you're saying. But you've got to tell her."

"I want to spare her the pain."

"How can you spare her the pain? Bro, it's too late for that. I warned you about Mary," Bryce says.

"But—"

"Deal with it. You're not the only one with problems." Then he sings, *"Mary, Mary got him hooked."*

Your phone rings again.

"She's had a crush on you since she was a little girl. She drew pictures of you in second grade. Your name and hers scrawled in crayon hearts. Oh, the way she spoke about you, and when we finally met *the* Poe Edgar Jackson—we fell in love with you too," her grandmother says.

"Yes, Mrs. C."

"Is it about race, Poe? Did some hateful person say something about Andrea being black?"

"Brown."

"What?"

"No, Mrs. C. It's not about race. Boo."

"You two are beautiful together."

"Yes, Mrs. C. Boo."

"Poe? Are you crying?"

"Yes, Mrs. C. Boo."

"Work it out with her."

"Yes, Mrs. Cohen. I'll try. Boo hoo. Boo hoo. Boo hoo."

12

The next call is from Tina.

"You're a loser. I don't know what Mary sees in you. And now you're in a love triangle?"

"Tina, why are you calling me?"

"To fuck with you, ass clown."

"But why?"

"You tried to touch my tits."

"No way. I was trying to give you that bear on a string."

"Hahaha. Who wants a stupid thing like that? You tried to touch my tits. You wanted to rape me like you did my girl in the car. That's right, she told me what you did, you rapist," Tina says.

"What! That's a lie. She came after me."

"Stay away from my girl!"

"You can have her!" you say.

"You're stuck with her! Ass clown."

Tina has a foul mouth and you hate her. Tina makes you so angry you just want to kill her. One day you probably will.

"Hold on." Tina passes the phone to someone laughing behind her.

"Hey, asshole." It's Jefferson.

"Hey, fuck head." It's Chucho, your weed man.

Tina's a rich girl, her parents own funeral homes, but she gets her weed from Chucho too.

Chucho says, "If you're done with Andrea, I'll take her."

Jefferson says, "Let me at them fat little tiddies."

Chucho says, "Oh, them tasty little tiddies."

The three of them sing, *"Ha ha, you can't have her. Ha ha, you can't have her. Ha ha, you can't have her."*

13

The next day is Saturday.

Valentine's Day.

The phone rings intermittently throughout the day, but you do not pick up. At 10:00 p.m. when it rings, you do not pick up. At 2:00 a.m. when it rings, it is Sunday, and you do not pick up. The phone does not ring after that.

You sulk all day Sunday.

By 8:00 p.m. you have made your decision.

You enter your mother's room, where she lies stretched out on the bed, snoring. Didn't even make it under the covers. Too tired. She has taken her medicine and won't awaken until morning when she will head off to her first job as a secretary at a law firm. Later that day she will take orders for eggs, pancakes, and coffee as a waitress at an all-night diner.

All of this to keep the lights on and a roof over your head, keep the Buick insured and its tank full of gas—she has done all of this to keep you from living an uncertain and precarious life in that blighted neighborhood of Pickett Park where children are born in abundance to live in cramped rooms and despair. This is how you repay her for all the hard work.

You cannot awaken her to tell her this. You cannot tell her this. She'll find out anyway after you've slit your own throat. She'll find out anyway when you're gone.

Why did you get out of the car that day? Why did you get out of the car? You can't understand why you got out of the car. You can't understand why you did it, but you did it.

You kiss your mother's forehead and whisper goodbye.

—Behind the house, you check the rattrap beneath the Buick parked above the hole in the ground where Dada kept his hunting tools.

Be silent. Listen. Dig the hole. Deposit the knives. Refill the hole. Mark the spot with a rattrap. Park the old car over the rattrap.

Dada was a genius. No one would think to look under an old car and under a rattrap, except rats.

There is a rat in the rattrap tonight.

He is injured, one paw caught in the powerful spring hammer. The paw is crushed. He won't use that paw again, no sir. Looks like he's gnawed at the hammer for a while and, making no progress, has given up. Rodent teeth, sharp as they are, aren't too effective against steel. Looks like he got tired of gnawing in futility at metal and has begun gnawing at his trapped limb. The white of bone is beginning to show. It must be painful, but it's better to be free with three paws than dead with four.

Carefully you liberate him from the trap. You wear heavy-duty gloves as a precaution, but he wouldn't bite you. If his rodent limbs were long enough, he'd hug you he's so grateful. For rats, human refuse is a free meal, human homes a place of warmth when it is cold. Rats know humans only set traps and kill them because they fear them.

You have no fear of rats. You set traps because their suffering delights you. It gets you through the hard times when others insult you, when they see you for what you are. Weird.

The rat thinks you want to make him a pet, the gentle way you rescued him from the trap—petting him and whispering soothingly. Rats know humans sometimes make them pets. This rat would like to be your pet.

If he only knew what's coming.

If he knew what's coming, he'd wish you'd left him in the trap to gnaw off his paw or die, for you have interesting ways of dealing with rats.

Interesting ways that are slow, and painful, and involve a dull razor—dull because it causes more suffering.

You are caught in a trap yourself, under an old car where no one would care to look. It's a good place to hide a broken heart. You are caught in a rattrap, held there by a paw you wish you could gnaw off, but you can't—you can't even suggest it to her, and if she suggested it to you, you'd say no. *Don't do it, Mary.* Children are precious.

I never had a brother or a sister and this child deserves a chance. If it's a boy we'll name him Poe, if it's a girl we'll name her Andrea . . .

You cry aloud, "How do I get out of this? What am I going to do? Dada, what am I going to do?"

You lift the dull razor, and the rat shivers.

After you slash the rat's throat, you will raise the dull razor and slash your own.

"Poe!"

—"Gross, dude," Bryce says.

You drop the rat, and it limps away. You slip the dull razor in its holster, pull off the gloves, and wash your hands with the backyard hose. Bryce throws his arms around you. You lay your head on his shoulder. Your best friend for life.

"I figured you were back here," he says.

"You came all the way over here?"

"Yeah, bro. Shouldn't have made that joke."

"Bryce."

"I'm thinking if it was me. You're only seventeen. I'm here for you, buddy."

He had said that before. Those exact words: *I'm here for you, buddy.*

You were ten. He was ten and a half. Playing on the roof of the abandoned warehouse in Pickett Park with some of his friends. You were told not to go to Pickett Park, but you would follow Bryce anywhere. And they were his friends, not yours. You had no friends. His friends didn't like you and they made it clear, but he brought you anyway.

Who invented the flying game? Fly from the roof of the abandoned warehouse and land safely on the stinky, torn-up mattress they had dragged from the dump.

Bryce's friends were angry that he had brought you. The fat kid. The booger picker. The kid with the bad daddy who had gone away. The fatty. The sissy.

When Bryce wasn't looking, they pushed you off the roof.

You weren't ready to fly. You missed the mattress completely. You landed facedown on the ground, your forehead bouncing like a basketball on the asphalt. The pain was magnificent and there was blood, though nothing was broken. The roof wasn't that high after all.

Their intent is what brought the tears. They didn't like you. They had wanted to hurt you.

There was a scream, then two, then three. You looked up. Bryce's friends were flying off the roof. Some landed on the mattress, but not all. All were crying, however.

One boy tried to escape down the ladder. Bryce pulled him back up, punched him, and pushed him off the roof. Bryce had punched all of them and thrown all of them off the roof. Bryce, the tough guy of the group, was sending a message: *No one messes with my best friend.*

He walked you home with his arm across your shoulder. You said, "You didn't have to."

He said, "It wasn't fair."

You said, "I'm used to it. I'm a punk."

He said, "Don't call yourself that."

You said, "I'm a sissy."

He said, "I'm here for you, buddy."

"Cool," you said, and touched his face.

He said, "Stop being weird," but did not flinch or move your hand away.

This night, he sits with you in the tree house Dada built for you, talking, crying, laughing sometimes at your half-hearted jokes.

And you think to yourself: *This night. This wonderful night is a bright spot in this dark period in my life because my buddy Bryce is here for me.*

Now it is he who touches your face. "Stop being weird," you say without pushing his hand away.

"I'm a sissy," he says.

You both laugh.

Then he says, "Can I sleep here tonight?"

"Sure!" you say. The night has just gotten better. Sleepovers with Bryce have always been fun.

Then he says, "Do you think there's a heaven?"

"Yes. I plan to go."

"I plan to go too, I guess." Then he says, "My parents caught me making out with a boy tonight. There was a fight. My mom was calming down after a while, it was sinking in for her, but Dad was blowing up. He hit me. I hit him back. He came at me and I slammed him to the ground. He was stunned that I would do that because I play football and I'm kinda strong and I had just told him I'm gay and he thinks that gays are weak, so he's all confused. I said, 'I'm getting out of here.' My mom said, 'You're just a kid, where will you go?' So, old buddy, can I stay here?"

You pause to let everything sink in. Bryce? Gay? You

used to shake your privates at him like maracas when you guys were small. Is that why he turned gay? Because of your little privates?

"Sure," you say after too long a while.

Then he's all jolly and confident again. "I'm just messing with you. I'm not gay," he says, and you get back to your miseries, your girlfriend who might dump you when she discovers your situation and your other girl who is pregnant, which is the situation.

And you and your best friend spend the night commiserating in your tree house until morning.

When you think back on that night, you'll wish you had said, *I'm here for you, buddy.*

14

The next day, you meet Andrea at her locker. You will try to work it out. You will try to explain, but she—

—She is overjoyed to see you.

She forgives you for the funny way you've been acting, and you know what else she wants to tell you? She loves you, that's what. She loves you, and no matter what you're going through that's making you act this way, she loves you. She is saying this to you as you stare at someone behind her.

She turns to see who it is behind her that intrigues you.

The ghoul is there. Tina stands next to her, holding her hand, grinning. Next to Tina are Jefferson and Chucho, your weed man, both grinning.

The ghoul is draped in a loose-fitting blouse with a basketball under it. Andrea wonders why you are focused on the ghoul.

The ghoul takes a step back. The loose-fitting blouse is from the maternity section at Kmart. The basketball is a baby. The ghoul is four months pregnant.

Andrea turns to you, a question on her face. *Is it yours?*

You nod.

How?

But now it makes sense to her. The nights you got there late. The nights you fell asleep early. The days you skipped school without her. The missed lunches. The missed—

She slaps your face.

* * *

—Andrea sniffs back tears as she unclasps your father's chain. She hands it back to you. "Take it."

"No." You won't take it.

You go to hold her, but the ghoul hooks your arm.

That's all she has to do. Hook your arm. Everyone can see that it has come full circle. Her vengeance is complete.

You want to hold Andrea, but the ghoul won't let you.

Who is Stupid Mary now? Stupid Andrea, stupid you, but not the ghoul. The ghoul may not be smart, but she is impressively wise. She is tremendously wise. She is unabashedly wise. The ghoul is wise beyond her years.

Andrea opens her hand. Dada's chain slips through her fingers and to the ground. The ghoul tells you to pick it up. You do, and she sets it in place around your neck and fastens the clasp while Andrea watches, pushing tears from her face. As she walks away through the parting crowd, everyone is laughing.

It's your fault. You did this. You promised you'd never hurt her. You promised you'd always protect her, but they are all laughing at her.

The loudest laughers are Jefferson and Chucho, your weed man.

—They are big, but you are bigger. There are two of them, but you bench 370.

Jefferson takes off down the hall.

Chucho, your weed man, attempts his escape in pants that droop below the waist, revealing scarlet boxers and the crack of his butt. He stumbles. You catch him. You get your hands around his throat. "I'm gonna fuck you up."

You give him a good beating and he spends a week in the hospital. Your suspension is a week and would've been longer, but you couldn't find Jefferson, though you tried.

—Bryce didn't come to school that day, too tired from the all-nighter in the tree house. When you called him that day from Mary's double-wide trailer, he was still alive.

You had a final chance to say it, but first you had to tell him all that happened with Andrea—how you loved her, how you had messed up, how you wanted her back, and he listened—so *I'm here for you, buddy* went unsaid.

Three days later in your backyard he was found swinging from a rope attached to his neck, the other end attached to the thick branch of the oak tree upon which your tree house was built.

He came to *your* backyard. He thought you'd be there. You were suspended from school, he thought you'd be at home, but you were in a double-wide trailer fucking Stupid Mary. You could've been there for him, but you weren't.

The suicide note Bryce left was not addressed to his parents, nor to his new best friend Muscle Teeth, whose tears at the funeral service were profuse, whose cries of grief coming from the back row of the church were heartrending, who walked out of the church before the service ended and did not appear at the graveside as his friend (boyfriend?) was interred. The suicide note Bryce left was addressed to *you*.

Is this the moment when empathy abandoned you?

2004

Bagging Carl Graham

"You wanted to know what it's about. That's what it's about. Carl, are you listening?"

Carl, who has been dead for an hour and twenty-seven minutes, does not answer.

The hunter drags Carl's corpse into the bathroom and places it in the tub where it settles gently. No more mason jars. No more cardboard boxes. Carl is his third and he has learned to do it right. The corpse will exsanguinate in the tub without doing further damage to the hardwood floor. This will make cleaning up easier.

When the corpse is drained, the hatchet and the carving knives are used to complete the dissection, and etc., and etc.

Though the hunter despises Carl, he leaves the arms attached because Carl is a talented piano player, the best he's heard. As a result of this concession to sentimentality, folding the torso to fit in the bag is tricky.

The flowers must go in his underwear, for Carl's pants have no pockets.

—After Carl's body parts are bagged, the hunter returns to the bathroom. He pours bleach in the tub where it will sit for twenty minutes.

In the living room, he opens the bag with his special mix of kitty litter and sand. He sprinkles it liberally on all of the contaminated surfaces. He pulls on his disposable gloves and gets down on his knees.

After the floor is spotless, he tackles the piano with soapy water and a damp white cloth. As he runs the cloth over the ivory keys, a noise like a sweet, aimless tune is produced. The high notes remind of the voices of children at play. The low notes remind of their voices when they are caught in mischief—the fear they feel just before you forgive them. High notes. Low notes. Notes in between. Children are precious.

He sprays air freshener in the air and on all of the surfaces he has just cleaned. He wipes everything down with Lysol and returns to the bathroom to see if the sitting bleach has done its job. It has. He scrubs the tub.

He loads his cleaning supplies in one bag. He drops the bloody napkins, special mix of kitty litter and sand, bloody rags, and disposable gloves in another. After his bags are packed, he showers and puts on a clean T-shirt. He scrubs the tub again.

Carl is fastidious about house care. There are no sheets to fold, no pillows to fluff, no dishes to wash.

—At the hospital, his wife's sisters wait in the lobby, each holding a fragrant bouquet of flowers. Cindy, Judy, Dixie, and Dottie, each one more beautiful than the one who came before. Their mother and boyfriend Roy are not there, though Roy left a cigar with Dottie, who embraces the hunter lovingly and says, "Congratulations, you're a father again!" On the sly her fingers brush against his crotch and she whispers in his ear: "When you're ready for a real celebration, I'm here."

—He enters the delivery room. His wife is in the final stage of pushing. Tina is there. "The ass clown cometh," Tina says.

His wife gesticulates wildly and snaps at him: "You're

wearing your pizza T-shirt? You left to go deliver pizza? You, you, you!"

"I said I'd be back in time and I am," says the hunter.

"Just barely," says Tina.

"You, you, you!" says his wife, as she descends into the mad incoherence of the final stage of pushing.

The hunter holds one hand, and Tina holds the other. The nurse tells her to push, push. The hunter's wife pushes one final time.

Then the baby comes, and it's a boy.

Victor Ulysses.

Compelled

It is two days later. It is 10:00 p.m.

The hunter is reluctant to leave the van and its powerful air conditioner, but out of the vehicle and into the sweltering heat he steps. It is the hottest July in ten years. How many powerful storms does this unbearable July heat portend? He is burning up as he makes a call from a phone booth outside a gas station on 57th near Opa Locka Airport.

"Be silent and listen," he says in his cracking old man's voice. He gives the location of Carl Graham's body. He adds: "His students are victims too. Consider how you failed *them* before you resume your relentless pursuit of me."

"And what about *you?*" a female voice asks. It is the same brown voice from Dr. David Perez. "Why do you do it?"

"Gomez was a wife beater. Perez was a wife stealer. Graham was a stealer of childhood innocence, a reprehensible pedophile. I am the exterminator of rats."

"I think you're more than that." There is a commotion behind her. They are not even trying to be quiet about tracing the call. But he enjoys her voice. He wishes he could meet her. In another life, maybe. She says, "You're hurting. I would like to help you."

"Help me by catching the Snatcher."

"You're not the Snatcher?"

"Come on. You must know that I'm not the Snatcher."

"You both use flowers. You both operate in July. You don't work together?"

"I don't work with rats," the hunter says.

"But I bet you know who he is, though. Do you?"

The question hangs in the air.

"Yes, I do."

"You do?! Tell us who he is!"

Sirens come screaming before the hunter can answer. He drops the phone and runs to the van.

In the van he says, "Maryanne Jamison."

That's what he would've answered.

Maryanne Jamison. A name he hasn't heard since 1999, but then Heidi mentioned it in her article.

Favorite Articles

At home, he writes his favorite journalist a letter:

> *I do not take my orders from a talking dog. The devil does not make me do it. I am not a psychopath. I am not a villain from a Poe story. In fact, I am perfectly sane.*

Some killers do that. They send messages to their favorite people in the press, and Heidi understands him, has understood him right from the beginning.

> *A hunter you wrote about, I admire. He shot his victims long range from highway overpasses in Virginia, Maryland, Delaware, and DC using a 1956 Savage 10FP high-powered rifle and scope, an ancient weapon, clunky and with questionable accuracy by today's standards, but he killed eleven people. Eleven people, seemingly at random. If they had known victim number three was his cheating wife, the hunter's spree would not have made it to four. I have given them Eduardo, David, and Carl. Have they figured out the pattern? Will I make it to Bob before they get me?*
>
>

Yours,
Periwinkle

He tears up the letter. He will call her instead.
"I'm away from my desk right now. Please leave a message at the sound of the tone."

"I am a tormented soul. If you are monitoring this call, pick up."

Heidi Renoir-Smith is writing a book on serial killers. He could help her with that, but she never picks up. Heidi is an excellent journalist who writes with a passion born of pain. Among the articles of hers he has committed to memory is the one on Richard Rogers.

Before real estate investor Richard Rogers set his 5-bedroom Harbor Beach "bungalow" on fire, killing his wife and her sister, he swapped their heads. Suzanne Green-Rogers's head was set in place on her sister Tabitha Green's neck, and the sister's head on Mrs. Green-Rogers's neck.

Rogers used a staple gun to attach the heads to the new bodies. His skill with the tool earned him the nickname "The Handyman."

Also found dead in the home were two men, Arnold Ray, 24, and Willie Farmer, 27, whose bodies were so badly burned and disfigured that identifying them as human was difficult.

Mrs. Green-Rogers's cat and dog were cut up and stapled in place in the men's stomachs. The cat's head was set on Arnold Ray's torso, the dog's head on Willie Farmer's.

During our interview, Rogers said: "Farmer kept coming at me even after I hurt him. I had to shoot him three times before he went down for good. He got the dog. Ray got the cat because he whined like a pussy all the way through it."

The human heads were set on the floor beneath the new velvet drapes and filled with kerosene. The fire started there.

An unflinching psychopath, Rogers calmly admitted to his crimes in court. Farmer and Ray were two drapery installers from a crew from McGill Fixers that had been hired to do renovations on the Harbor Beach property last month. Farmer and Ray were young, fit, and African American.

Rogers, 75, had observed the attention his much younger wife, Suzanne Green-Rogers, 30, and her unmarried sister, Tabitha Green, 28, gave the men, and it angered him.

"I thought she and her sister were banging them," Rogers said.

After Rogers shot them, he used their own staple gun to complete the job.

Rogers "The Handyman" struck four more times before he was caught. His final victims were two prostitutes, a homeless man, and a cabdriver.

In court he said, "I almost made it to Mexico, but I turned back. These last four? I didn't even know them. I did it on impulse."

—"Bravo, Richard! Bravo!"

Rogers shares the hunter's jealousy, his rage, his sense of justice.

—In his Carl notes he writes, *With such talent, he could've given so much to the children. Instead, he preyed on them.*

—That night, he dreams about Bob.

In the dream Bob has no hands. He doesn't have to be told that Bob is ready, but Dada says it anyway.

Bob is ready.

I
DISAPPEARED
HIM

JULY 1999–JULY 2004

Junior

It was a boy!

He was their firstborn, so they named him Poe Edgar Jr.

And she refused to accept his proposal of marriage, and he told her that Junior needed a father, and she said that she needed someone who could make love to her and mean it, and he said that he would, and she said: "You'll fake it."

And he said, "I won't fake it."

And she said, "You always fake it. You're faking it now."

And he said, "I'm not faking. I've got things on my mind."

And she said, "The only reason you want to marry me is because you believe that a strong, independent woman can't raise a child without a man."

And he said, "I fully believe that you are capable of raising Poe Jr. without a man, but I want to be in his life."

And she said, "You can be in his life on weekends. But I don't need or want you in my house. Furthermore, you do not love me and I do not love you."

And he said, "But we can learn to love each other."

And she said, "You were gone three days. I smelled her on you."

And he said, "I do not have a girlfriend."

And she said, "You should get one."

And he said, "I love you."

And she said, "I have a boyfriend.

And he said, "Tell me his name."

And she said, "I'm pregnant again. I think it's his."

And he said, "You're just like your sisters."

He rolled off her.

He got up and put on his clothes. After a while she did too. They sat on the edge of the bed fully dressed, silent in their own thoughts, his dark and melancholic, hers defiant and blissfully ignorant. She refused to tell him her lover's name.

He stalked her until he found out.

It was Bob the dry cleaner.

A brown man.

2

Bob Montgomery sensed more rage in the man stomping toward him than he cared to handle in front of customers on Sunday, the busiest washday of the week.

Bob was the handsome owner of Round the Clock Laundromat and Dry Cleaning. He was stylishly dressed in a red silk shirt, a matching headband, and white sneakers with sensible heels.

It had to be about a woman.

Some men get lazy after they marry. They stop dressing to attract. They lose interest in personal hygiene and grooming. They stop telling her, *You are beautiful. I'm glad that you are mine.* They forget she had a life before them. They stop seeing her as a person until Bob the handsome, well-dressed dry cleaner makes a play.

The day she moved out, Bob's wife had warned: "One day someone's husband is going to come after you and you're gonna get it."

Presently Bob was juggling four of them. One whose husband was considerably older and condescended. He didn't argue trifles with her, dismissed her antics as childish, even when he came home one day and she had painted the living room black—painted the couch, the expensive shag carpet, the walls, the windows, the dog. "Like a child crying out for attention," he dismissed without anger.

Bob said, "The painted *dog* didn't get his attention?"

The cuckold's wife said, "I told him I was having an affair. He told me, 'Enjoy yourself.'"

"He doesn't deserve you."

The second, a woman he had been with for five years, was married to an accountant who spent twelve hours a day at the office. The first time Bob took her, it was in the back on a tumble dryer that needed repair. She tallied her orgasms on a balance sheet she took from her husband's office and faxed it back to Bob: *As you can see from these numbers, all accounts are settled. You put me in the black. Or should I say, put the black in me.*

They had a good laugh over her clever play on words.

One had a lover whose youthfully vigorous and kinky sex she enjoyed. But he was immature. He berated her in public. He called her fat. He lived off her earnings.

Bob called her his cherry blossom, told her she smelled like sunshine, and asked her as they undressed, "Don't lie. He's stronger, right? But can he do this?" He kissed her neck in that special way. With feeling. Touched her where it meant the most. In her heart. After they finished, they smoked a joint and he held her until they were foul enough to need a bath. In the shower he said, "See, the young guys have more energy. They pump and pump. It's all for their ego, not *your* pleasure. They hardly think about you. I'm thirty-nine, just a big ole teddy bear. But I'm tender, and I can go all night for you."

His crown jewel lived with a pizza man. She had given up a tennis scholarship to have their child.

While her muscle-bound wimp of a boyfriend worked for tips, she held down three part-time jobs—as a receptionist at her best friend's family's funeral home, as a private singing coach at home and sometimes at her old high school, and at the community center as a music teacher to underprivileged children.

He told her, "I would give up all this for you. My money,

my possessions. You're the most wonderful woman I have ever met. You're intelligent. You're beautiful. Your eyes! They are blue and gray as a storm at sea. If I'm not careful I'll drown in them."

She was an impressive beauty and fertile, this one. He wouldn't mind getting her pregnant. Their child would be the most beautiful of all his children, even more so than Mary-anne.

He spotted the Munchie Luciano's Pizza van and quickly ran behind the counter.

Bob raised the telephone. "I'll call the police."

The hunter stepped inside. "Call them," he said, and leaped over the counter.

—Bob was a big man and heavy. With some effort, he fought out of the choke hold and ducked down. He got his hand on the base of the old-fashioned phone, which had fallen, swung it up, and connected with the hunter's face.

Shrugging off the blow, the hunter tackled him. They rolled on the ground where the hunter's rage gave him the advantage. Bob was bleeding badly, and he wasn't hitting back. The crazed pizza man kept slamming his fists down on the well-dressed dry cleaner's head. Bob's sin of taking another man's wife was inconsequential. Taking another man's wife was a mere peccadillo of a crime—on the books true, but winked at by the courts. Many seduced other men's wives, but why his? Anyone's but his.

Another blow.

Another blow.

It took four customers—two for each arm—to pull the hunter off their handsome dry cleaner.

Terms

For assaulting his wife's lover, the hunter spent the night in jail. His mother borrowed the five hundred dollars for bail from her office manager at the law firm where she worked part-time as a secretary.

Vince let him sleep on a mattress in the back of the pizzeria where the unfolded boxes were stacked. His eyes wet, he called his wife.

"I want to come home."

"You've got to apologize to Bob."

"You're crazy."

"You've got to tell him you're sorry."

"For what, beating his ass?" he said.

"I love you both. I want you both," she said.

"You are trash," he said. "Just like your mother and your sisters, pure trash, and I'm done with you."

Junior began crying, and she left to go tend to him.

Fifteen minutes she was gone. He thought about what he would say when she came back. He thought about hanging up, but didn't. Twenty minutes. Twenty-seven. Thirty-one minutes.

When she came back, an hour and five minutes later, she said, "You're still on the line, I see."

"You were testing me."

"Actually, I forgot you were here."

"You were testing me, and you won. I love you."

She laughed her sweet laugh. "Under all of that muscle,

you're a nice guy. He's nice too. He's better to talk to. You're better in bed. You're like two sides of the same coin. I want the whole coin." Then switching to a child's voice, she added, *"Mommy, gimme the whole quarter, pweese."*

"My God, you're trash."

"I bring in more money. I'm better educated. I have a 3.5 average at the community college while taking care of the baby. Why don't you try taking classes, you Science Club nerd, you bully? *You're* the trash, you pizza man."

"Trash."

"If you call me trash again, I'll go back and fuck Bob."

"Trash," he said.

She hung up.

"That's fine," he said to the dead line.

He got up from the mattress and stepped into his slippers. She was right. She was right about everything she said. She made more money, but he worked hard too. He could take classes at the community college too if he wanted, but he didn't have time for school anymore. There were things on his mind. Things the dark thoughts were telling him to do. Things he was preparing to do. He passed through the restaurant where the tables were set up. He ended at the glass window at the storefront. It was late at night and the pizza van sat alone in the parking lot. He was alone . . . but he was the better parent, damn it! He never yelled at Junior or put his hand on him like she sometimes did. He found a rag in the supplies closet, squirted liquid soap into a pail of water, and washed every inch of the window so clean he could see his face in it. It was not a happy face. Was that tear from anger or from sadness? He dropped the rag in the pail and got the broom and swept the floor. He considered polishing the floor as a cure for his loneliness, but what was the use?

Separate and apart on most things they were, but on this they agreed: love means never having to sleep alone when you're suicidal.

She was alone too, or was she?

He went back to the storage room. He took off his slippers and stretched out on the mattress with the phone in his hand. He dialed for an hour.

Maybe Bob's fucking her right now. If he's there fucking her, I'm gonna tear him apart this time.

He stepped into his shoes and grabbed the keys to the van, but the phone rang.

"Don't talk to me like that ever again. Don't call me trash. I know what I come from, but it hurts." It was quiet in his home behind her. Her voice didn't quaver. "He's afraid of you. He's scared to go to work thinking you'll show up again. He could press charges. They could send you to jail."

"Just kiss and make up like two kids, huh?"

"Say you're sorry."

"This is not kindergarten." Poe was nobody's fool—she'd cucked him. But he was a weak man. He loved her. Maybe Bob loved her too. Two sides of the same coin, she had said. Maybe Bob was a weak man too. "Okay," Poe said. "I'll call and tell him whatever you want me to, but I can't promise I won't go after him if I see him around you."

"You're a bully," she said.

"Don't go to his dry cleaners anymore."

"It's a free country," she said.

"Are you crazy? Those are my terms." The tears were salty in his mouth, and he choked on them. "It hurts," he said. "It hurts."

—While his wife listened in on the three-way line, the hunter begged the brown man who may have impregnated her for forgiveness and promised he wouldn't come after him, but he added: "Understand this, if you go near her again—"

"I get it," said Bob. "I get it."

"Oh, you'll get it," the hunter said. "You'll get it."

"Okay. Okay," Bob said, laughing.

He laughed.

He Laughed

As he waited in the empty parking lot across the street from Round the Clock Laundromat and Dry Cleaning, the peppermint gum turned to powder in his mouth.

On Wednesdays, Bob always took his lunch break at 1:00. The hunter pushed another stick of peppermint gum into his mouth without spitting out the powder of the first. Now he had fat gum in his mouth. He liked the taste and feel of the fat gum in his mouth. It was like adding life to a dead thing. Stick after stick. Gum after gum. Rat after rat. He checked his watch: 1:35. Maybe something was wrong. Maybe he should leave and come again tomorrow.

There was movement at the front of the store. The doors opened and Bob and another man came out, a brown man shorter than Bob, and thin with a goatee. The other man was Jack, the assistant manager.

In a loud voice, Bob scolded the shorter man for a mistake he had made in the ordering of detergent. There was some talk of the man losing his job for the mistake. The shorter man took it meekly. When Bob finished with him, the other guy went back inside. Bob went to his Lexus.

Bob the handsome well-dressed playboy with this prosperous business had the power to chastise a grown man in public, to threaten his livelihood even. Bob had that fancy car he didn't deserve. Bob had had his wife. Probably still had her.

He's gonna get it today.

Over the month that he'd been stalking Bob, he learned

that the handsome dry cleaner always took a lunch of two to three hours. He always spent it with one of the women he was seeing.

Bob's home, where he took the women for "lunch," was due south, but his Lexus drove due north on I-95. The hunter thought he knew all of Bob's women. Maybe Bob had a new woman. Bob was prodigious, but can a man handle more than three women? Four. The hunter's wife used to be in that mix. Maybe still was. Bob was a playboy. Bob was a whore. He screwed the hunter's wife and laughed. Brushing him off.

The hunter does not take a brush-off lightly.

Traffic was light and Bob had a heavy foot. The hunter in his old Buick rattled behind him. They passed 79th Street. The Lexus stretched the distance between them. The hunter surged over sixty, sixty-five, over seventy, keeping him in sight. The Lexus, zooming over eighty, ninety, was soon out of sight.

Blue and red lights flashed up ahead. Traffic slowed. A police stop.

Bob?

When the hunter arrived at the flashing lights, it wasn't Bob's Lexus that had been pulled over, but a Mercedes. Inside the car was a brown boy, maybe eighteen with dreadlocks and bright but sad eyes. A brown girl of the same age was next to him in the passenger seat, smoking a cigarette.

The hunter caught up to Bob's Lexus as it exited the highway at 119th Street. Bob put on his blinkers, made a left onto 119th. Ahead of him were a KFC, a Winn-Dixie, and Eladios's barbershop where the hunter went to get his hair cut. Bob made a right onto Seventh Avenue. He drove north until he reached 135th where he made another left. The hunter followed at a distance. Bob drove west on 135th until he reached a neighborhood of modest homes.

The girlfriend must live here. I'll put her in a closet, save her from watching him get it. If I can't get her in a closet, I'll smack him around some more right in front of her. Show her what kind of a punk he is. Spend another few nights in lockup. Probably go to jail. Won't see the kid for a couple of years. This is a bad plan. Maybe I should rethink this.

Across the street from the modest neighborhood was a cemetery. Bob's Lexus pulled into the cemetery.

The hunter parked outside the entrance to the cemetery, North Dade Memorial Gardens, and waited. So that Bob wouldn't spot him, he waited ten minutes longer than he needed before pulling in. The cemetery was vast. It took fifteen minutes to find Bob at a grave in a section of the park called "Serenity."

Bob's eyes were closed. His lips moved as if in prayer. When he finished his prayer, he pulled up some weeds, swept them into a small lawn bag. He cleared away the dead flowers and set fresh ones in their place. White roses, chrysanthemums, lilies, hyacinths, red roses. When the fresh flowers were in place, he went back to his Lexus and drove away.

The hunter did not follow him. He went to the grave and read the headstone:

Maryanne Jamison
(Sunrise June 7, 1989–Sunset July 17, 1999)

Little Brown Zoe

He clung to hope. There was still a chance the baby was his.

Back at home, a month became two months, and two months became three, and three months became the ninth month, and the baby was born.

It was a girl!

Zoe Yasmine Jackson, her birth certificate read. Where it said *Father* was his name: *Poe Edgar Jackson.* The hospital staff chuckled knowingly. That last name didn't change the fact that Zoe Yasmine Jackson was brown.

The night his wife came back from the hospital with little brown Zoe in her arms, he drank his first beer for the pleasure of being sad or whatever it was that people drank beer for. He hated the taste of beer and only drank when she did so she wouldn't drink alone. He spat it out.

He went to his mother's backyard and freed an injured rat from the trap under the old car. One of the rat's legs was crushed. He named it Bob and sliced its face off.

He didn't understand the purpose of beer and he didn't like the taste. Watching a rat struggling to find its way on three legs with no face—he understood the purpose of that completely.

—His wife apologized. He said he forgave.

Her to him: twenty Kit Kat chocolate bars arranged like a bouquet of flowers. Kit Kat was no longer his favorite candy bar. He had told her this a year ago.

Him to her: a makeup kit. "Makeup Kit for the make-up," she said, feigning joy when she unwrapped it.

"Make-up sex would've been better, but you're still gimpy from having his bastard," he said back.

"Fuck you," she said.

"That's the point," he said. "Fuck me. Fuck me. I'm fucked. That's the point exactly."

Her to him: a ticket to see his favorite movie, *Titanic*. She found the movie overhyped and dull, so he went alone. He shed tears in the dark theater, his hand on the empty seat next to him, remembering Andrea and what he once hoped might've been.

Him to her: a rickety secondhand washing machine from Handyman Ricky Hardware Store so that she'd have no reason to go to Bob's.

Her to him: an oath—"I promise to be true to you from now on."

Him to God: an oath—"Bob is gonna get it."

—A year became two, and two became three, and it was 2004.

Eduardo was gone. David was gone. Carl was gone.

E, D, C. I disappeared them in preparation for this.

Every day he was reminded that Zoe, who was three, was not his by blood. He was humiliated but she was his child and he loved every brown inch of her.

Red and yellow, brown and white, they are precious in His sight—Sunday school, cardboard forts, a box of Cracker Jacks with a toy inside. All of it!

BROWN-HEADED COWBIRD

Bob

July 17, 2004

Bob lives on a quiet street in the design district. His Spanish mission–style home, which sits on property that is well lit, is modest for a man of his means. The hunter arrives early to disconnect the backyard lights. Then he settles into the murky darkness to wait.

At 1:30 a.m., Bob's late-model Lexus pulls in under the freestanding limestone archway on the side of his home that he uses as a carport. When he steps out of the car, the big man is dressed in a red polo shirt, pleated black jeans, and comfortable, velvet, hard-toe work shoes.

The well-dressed dry cleaner peers into the dark backyard. He frowns. The lights are out again, but he is tired from standing on his feet all day, his comfortable shoes notwithstanding. All he wants is a hot shower and a warm bed.

It is a safe street in an upscale neighborhood. Bob inserts the key in the lock and pushes open the door.

—When the hunter enters through the main bedroom's window, he hears the shower running in the bathroom.

For a man so well dressed, Bob keeps a nasty home. On the bed where they made love, loose socks of various hues and underwear of various stages of cleanness are stacked in a pile and pushed to one side. More dirty laundry dangles from the drawers and spills from the closets. The sheet is stained with something dark that may have once been red. Perhaps Bob ate spaghetti last night.

The hunter never eats food in bed. The hunter never leaves clothes unwashed, unfolded, and scattered about. The hunter is fastidious. The hunter is a neat freak. He washes and folds. He slips a stick of gum in his mouth and waits.

—With a black towel wrapped around his midsection and fuzzy, open-toe slippers on his feet, Bob comes out of the bathroom.

He sees the hunter and his eyes go wide. "Wait," he says.

The hunter punches with the blade, but Bob slips it.

He punches again and catches air. Bob grabs his wrist. The hunter is strong, but Bob is strong too. Since his beating, he has been spending time in the gym. The hunter is surprised to find himself slung off, crashing violently against the wall.

Bob ducks down. He reaches under the bed and comes up with a stainless steel wrench with a weirdly shaped head, a menacing weapon longer than his forearm. Bob swings the wrench, and the breeze whistles across the hunter's face as the heavy tool just misses.

"*En garde*," Bob says, and swings the wrench again. For a big man, Bob is light on his feet. He makes a quick rooster step to the right, then left, and swings the wrench in a wide arc. It connects this time.

The blow knocks the hunter to the ground. He is on his hands and knees. His nose is broken. The gum has been knocked out of his mouth. He is stunned from the blow. He climbs unsteadily to his feet. He opens his hand. His empty hand. Where did it go?

Bob holds up the rapier. "Looking for this?" he says.

The hunter is winded and his vision is blurred, but Bob is advancing, coming toward him.

"*En garde*," Bob says, and he jabs with the rapier.

The hunter rolls away from the strike. The blade catches his shoulder, and stumbling in Bob's messy, disorganized room, his feet get tangled in the clutter of clothes and he slips. He falls forward on his face.

On hands and knees again, the blood flowing like syrup from his broken nose, he hears Dada say: *Fix it.*

He shakes his head, snorting and blowing like a bull, clearing the blood from his nose, clearing his head. He is able to see straight again.

Bob is laughing at him, still advancing. The rapier is in one hand. The towel around his waist is held up by the other hand. Where is the wrench?

Over there by the messy bed! Dada says.

The hunter scrambles across the carpet and grabs the wrench, which lies at the foot of the messy bed. In one fluid movement, he shoots up and lays the heavy steel wrench across Bob's face.

Bob's big body sways unsteadily. Then it collapses and hits the ground with a loud thud.

Dada applauds. *Fix it. Fix it.*

The hunter stands over Bob, raises the heavy wrench above his head, and brings it down. There is a resounding crack as something essential in Bob's face breaks.

The hunter, who has never beaten a man to death, is uncertain what part of Bob's face has been broken by the stainless steel wrench. He recalls the Latin words *maxilla*, *mandible*, *malar*, and *occipital* he crammed for a biology test. He takes the rapier from Bob's hand and with it massages the broken *malar* bone (also know as the *zygomatic* arch or cheekbone) to see if he is conscious. The dead man coughs and three teeth jump from his mouth.

—The hunter says to Bob, "Where's the boy?"

"F-fuu."

The dead man's jaw, the *maxilla*, is broken and crunches when he tries to speak. His words are indecipherable. The hunter leans closer.

"What did you say?"

"F-fuck you," Bob says.

He punches Bob's face. It's like punching raw meat.

"Where's the boy?"

Bob's left eye is undamaged and remains open. The undamaged left eye is fixed on the hunter. It is the eye of someone sneering. In that respect, it seems out of place in Bob's broken face. If Bob could sneer, the eye would not seem out of place. Bob's jaw crunches and clicks, and a sound issues forth from the twisted mouth. The sound is rhythmic, huffing. Bob is not dead. Bob is laughing.

The hunter punches the meat face again, but no answer from the man with the sneering eye. Bob's jaw crunches and clicks. He continues to laugh.

Bob is naked, the towel wrapped around his waist having fallen. Beneath the mountainous stomach, the sad little organ that engendered Zoe is exposed. It lies coiled, bare, and unprotected. The hunter taps it with the rapier.

"Where is the boy?"

The eye in the undamaged orbital (eye socket) slowly closes. The broken jaw crunches. "H-hh . . . ivivvng hhroom."

"The living room?"

Bob's jaw clicks. "Yhhhehhh."

"Where in the living room?"

Bob's jaw crunches. "Hhh-V."

"The TV?"

Crunch. "Hhh-V."

"In the TV?"

Click. "Nnn."

"Then where?"

Crunch. Crunch. "Clahhzzt, pessihzt."

"What?" the hunter says.

Crunch. Crunch. "Clahhzzt, pessihzt."

The hunter holds up a hand. "Never mind. I'll figure it out."

The blade's first strike is to the *maxilla*, which is the upper jaw. There follow sixteen more strikes, seventeen in all, pulverizing the Latinized bones.

But Bob is dead after the first strike.

Four by Four by Four

Bob's living room is the only clean room in the house. On the walls are hung a few paintings of flowers. White roses and lilies mostly. There is a big-screen TV on the wall above a stark white couch with expensive throw pillows.

There are other chairs in the room, but the hunter stares at the white couch. Something about that arrangement bothers him.

Right, says Dada. *Why put the TV on the wall behind the couch? What do you do, twist your neck around to watch it?*

Next to the couch is a tall wicker cabinet with a candlestick lamp sitting on the top shelf. The hunter pulls the couch away from the wall and pushes the wicker cabinet aside, carefully so as to keep the candlestick lamp from falling. There is a small door hidden behind the tall cabinet.

Good boy, Dada says.

Padlocked and built into the innards of the house, whatever is behind the door is only slightly more secure than a cabinet used to hide cleaning products from children.

One padlock.

"Is this the best you can do, Bob?"

The hunter was expecting more than this and is armed with a bolt cutter, which he uses.

He opens the door and is met by a sealed steel closet.

He's smart, Dada says. *But you're smarter. Come on, son.*

The steel closet is four feet by four feet by four feet. It is built into the concrete wall, so there is no way to get behind it.

Come on, son. Think. Think.

He could break through the wall, but he'd have to drive an hour to his mother's to get the sledgehammer.

From the four air holes drilled in the top of the steel closet comes a huffing sound.

Breathing.

—He passes a hand over the surface of the steel door riveted to the front of the steel closet.

There are twenty rivets. With his fingers, he inspects each smooth, perfectly set rivet; one, two, three, four, five, six, seven, eight, nine, ten, eleven, twelve, thirteen, fourteen, fifteen, sixteen, seventeen—the seventeenth rivet gives a little.

He positions the heavy bolt cutter against number seventeen. He digs at it, but the bolt cutter slips. Rivet number seventeen is loose but like the other nineteen perfectly smooth.

The breathing from within the box becomes more vigorous. Now there is movement. Kicking?

"Don't worry. I'm here now," he says into the holes.

For five minutes, he attacks each rivet with the bolt cutter. No good. Not one of them yields. They are too deeply planted.

He needs a better tool. He needs . . . He could kick himself. He needs the wrench with the weird head.

He runs to Bob's bedroom for the stainless steel wrench. In seven minutes, he has removed the twenty smooth rivets and dragged the heavy steel door out of the way.

A puff of warmth from the open doorway caresses his face with the stench of urine and feces. He slaps a hand over his mouth.

He has seen many things. But this?

The prisoner lies on his side on the bare steel floor. He is shirtless, bound hand and foot, with a black bandanna tied over his eyes and a gag in his mouth. The prisoner is a ten-year-old brown boy.

The foul stench in the steel container comes from the urine and feces that have seeped through the boy's pants.

Brown Boy

The hunter says to the brown boy lying on his side in the steel prison, "I'm going to remove the gag over your mouth so you can breathe. Don't scream."

I won't, the boy indicates by shaking his head.

The hunter removes the gag. The boy lets out a ragged breath and sucks in a great gulp of air. The hunter puts a hand on this back, steadying him.

"Take your time. You're free. Breathe. Breathe."

When the boy stops heaving, the hunter undoes the extension cord that binds his legs together. He pulls him up and guides him carefully through the steel doorway so that he doesn't bang his head against the frame or cut his bare feet on the sharp threshold. He seats the brown boy on the couch and goes to the refrigerator for a bottle of water.

When the hunter returns, he says to the boy: "I brought you some water."

The boy is soft-voiced and polite. "Thank you, sir. I'm very thirsty."

The extension cord binding his hands is tight. He tries to move his hands, and cries out as it pinches his wrists: "Ouch! Ouch!"

The hunter loosens the extension cord but does not free his hands completely, for he doesn't want him to make a sudden move. "That should feel better," the hunter says. Then he holds the water bottle to the boy's mouth.

In big gulps, he drinks his fill.

"Are you Jermaine?"

The boy nods. "Yes sir. Are you the police?"

"No."

"Are you a fireman?"

"No."

"Are you going to hurt me?"

"No."

"Then why can't I take the thing off my eyes?" Jermaine begins crying softly. "Mommy. I want my mommy. Please, mister, I want my mommy."

"You'll see her soon. You'll see her tonight," the hunter says. His bleeding scars, the welts on his back—he's been through enough, and he calms somewhat at the hunter's words. The hunter touches a gentle finger to the scars.

The brown boy winces.

"Sorry," the hunter says.

"It's okay."

"I'll look for some food," the hunter says.

The brown boy's voice is weak and dry-sounding despite the water. "No food. He took me out of the box to feed me. Then he spanked me hard. He said I was a bad boy. He said he could spank me. He said he was trying to be a good daddy."

"No daddy would do this. He's a bad daddy," the hunter says.

Heaving and shaking as he weeps, the brown boy really lets go. The hunter wraps him in his arms. After a while, the boy's shaking subsides. The hunter places a hand on his shoulder where there are no welts.

"You gotta eat, Jermaine."

Jermaine shakes his head. "No sir."

The hunter insists, "You're hungry."

He goes to the kitchen. In the refrigerator there is a plastic container. He lifts the lid and finds leftover spaghetti. He sniffs it to see if it's still good, then microwaves a plateful and brings it back to Jermaine, who eats ravenously from a fork held to his mouth by the hunter.

"Not hungry, huh?" As Jermaine devours the spaghetti, the hunter chuckles. With four children of his own, the hunter knows that sometimes you've got to make them eat, no ifs, ands, or buts. Tough love works.

Bagging Bob

Tonight he has brought with him the six eighty-gallon heavy-duty reusable garden waste bags he purchased yesterday at Home Depot.

The eighty-gallon heavy-duty garden waste bags come in packs of three. Each pack costs $23.75 with taxes. For Bob, who is a big man, he purchased two packs for just in case.

In the end, bagging Bob uses only one pack of bags. The hunter mourns the $23.75 wasted on the second pack.

Flowers for Dead Children

Under Bob's bed, the hunter discovers a photo album containing page after page of pressed flowers. Gladiolas, carnations, chrysanthemums, orchids, white roses.

Funeral flowers, Dada tells him, *taken from their graves.*

"It's a swap. He puts a lily in their hand after he . . . kills them. He takes the best of what is left by other people at their graves," the hunter says. "I followed him to the little girl's grave. Maryanne Jamison. I remembered the name from an article Heidi wrote back when I was in high school. Maryanne was a Snatcher victim. I followed him there to kill him, but he was grieving a child. We both have a fondness for children, so my heart went out to him. You never gave me any brothers or sisters."

Dada says, *But I gave you love. That counts for something. Love from a father to a son means everything.*

"You were the best father. Bob was a father too. If he was Maryanne's blood father, it made sense to me that he was there," the hunter says. "If my child were a Snatcher victim, my grief would be as heavy. A week later, I followed him to the resting place of Billy McWhorter, another Snatcher victim. My mind raced. Two children. Two Snatcher victims. Could it be? Over the next few months he visited them all. He went to the graves of other children who weren't reported in the news as Snatcher victims."

Above the funeral flowers on each page, a name is written in purple crayon: *Robin, Tobias, Suzy, Chuck, Morgan,*

Billy, Maryanne, Jermaine, Zoe . . . There are no flowers on Jermaine's or Zoe's page. He never got to murder them.

Dada says, *He visits them boldly to sweep their graves. He removes the dead flowers and replaces them with fresh ones. Seemingly put there at random, a bouquet of lilies is always there among the fresh flowers. Oh, the thrill he must feel, hiding in plain sight. To the groundskeepers he appears to be just another grieving family member, and he is. He is their father.*

"The next few years, he lay dormant. I checked the news every day. And then Jermaine."

You see, he blames the children for what he is. Visiting their graves may be a sign of genuine remorse. He may have genuinely loved them. I would've done the same if I had murdered you.

The hunter remains silent out of respect. On this one point he disagrees with Dada. Visiting their graves is not a sign of remorse, genuine or otherwise. Bob is a monster. Visiting their graves is the part of the ritual where he collects his trophies. He keeps the best of the dead flowers in this album in this filthy room, stashed under his bed.

But none of that matters now, for he had promised Bob was going to get it, and Bob got it. Bob is a dead man.

If the hunter had to give Bob a name, it would be "The Mourner" or perhaps "The Cemetery Man" or "The Brown-Headed Cowbird," a species of bird that inserts its eggs in another bird's nest to be raised by her.

My Hero

After Bob's place has been put back together and the hunter takes his shower and cleans the shower, he drives Jermaine to a corner near his home and lets him out of the van. He carefully removes the extension cord that binds his hands, but leaves the blindfold in place. He tells Jermaine: "Count to fifty before you take the blindfold off. Can you do that?"

Jermaine wraps his arms around the hunter's waist. "But you're a hero."

The hunter leans down for a better hug. He puts his face to the boy's face. "I'm not a hero, Jermaine."

The hunter climbs into the van, and Jermaine begins to count. He gets to thirty-one and rips the blindfold off. He wants to see his hero.

The van is already gone.

This Has Never Happened Before

The hunter arrives home to his small apartment, and his wife is on the settee in a housecoat and her favorite silver slippers, watching TV. An Alka-Seltzer commercial is playing. *"Plop, plop, fizz, fizz, oh what a relief it is."* She looks up at him and with a creaky effort gets up slowly from the couch. There is a look of exhaustion on her face.

"Late night, huh?" she says.

"You okay?"

"I'm okay," she says. "What happened to your nose?"

He covers the broken nose with a hand. "Accident at work."

"Pizza accident."

"Yes."

She yawns and turns back to the TV. The program is back on, something with a dog and boy, but not *Old Yeller*. Something about the end of the world. "I heard sirens," she says. "Somebody got shot down the street. I waited up for you."

He opens his mouth, but the words *I had to go to the warehouse* die on his lips as she clicks off the TV and goes into the bedroom.

He had been expecting a fight. There is no fight. He won't have to spend tonight's tips on a hotel.

He goes into the bathroom to see about his nose. There's a swelling and it leans too much to one side. It's broken. There is a sharp pain as he holds it between his thumbs and snaps it back in place. He takes eight Motrin tablets for the pain and leaves the bathroom. He checks on the kids, who're sleeping soundly. He kisses little brown Zoe on the forehead before heading to his bedroom and getting into bed with his wife whose eyes are still open. She has recently given birth, but she takes his erection in her hand.

"It's one of those nights, huh?"

"Yes," he says.

"There are things we can do if we're careful."

She smacks her lips and makes a sexy sound at the back of her throat. He doesn't know if the sound is for him or Bob. Bob. Ha. He clicks off the lights and turns on his side, facing her. She kisses his mouth. He puts his arm over her in preparation. She adjusts her body. She has recently given birth, but she is eager to receive her pleasure.

"Be careful," she says.

"I'll be careful."

"Don't be careful. Be good."

He says nothing.

"Poe?" his wife says.

But the hunter is more exhausted than horny and has fallen asleep in the middle of their game. This has never happened before.

Bueno Bye

The hunter sleeps until noon.

After breakfast, he washes the dishes. He sets the pot on the stove and starts cooking tonight's meal. He spends an hour giving the apartment a general cleaning. He takes the trash down to the incinerator. Last night was a good kill. His wife stays out of his way when he gets like this, furiously cleaning, cooking, muttering to himself.

When the baby cries, he takes him from her arms and changes him. Then he checks the pot. Tonight there will be curry chicken. He stirs the mix of garbanzo beans, onions, chunks of potatoes, and yellow curry simmering in the pot.

When the cooking is done, he goes back to Bob's to spend more time with that messy bedroom. When the bedroom is in order, he removes the sheets from the dryer and folds them. He scrubs the white carpet again to ensure that all signs of blood are erased. He tidies up and does some dusting. He whistles while he works. In an hour and a half he is finished.

As he drives away from Bob's house, he passes a caravan of police cruisers with their lights blinking, going in the opposite direction. They are headed to Bob's house.

"That was fast. Jermaine must've told them."

After work, he makes the trip to the Everglades. He spots the two police cruisers before they spot him and keeps on driving.

"They await me at the dump site as though I'm that stupid," the hunter says. "Ah, if I *were but* that stupid. Tehehe."

He considers driving farther north into Collier County, where there is another entrance to the Everglades, but cops will likely be posted there too.

Bob's flesh is beginning to stink in the eighty-gallon heavy-duty garden waste bags, even though they are the scented ones guaranteed to eliminate odor. He can't wait another day. For the first time, he will use a backup site.

He takes the Palmetto Expressway north, past middle-class Palmetto Grove where he grew up, to Pickett Park where he lives now in the shadow of a mound of trash.

In the dark of the night, he uses the wire cutters and enters the Palmetto Cove Municipal Solid Waste Transfer Site, the towering landfill that everyone calls Mt. Trash-More.

Mt. Trash-More is an appropriate place to disappear a piece of wife-stealing trash like Bob.

Bueno bye, Bob.

Two Sides of the Same Coin

There are only four picture frames in the hunter's small apartment. In one picture frame, the silver one on the nightstand on his side of the bed, there is a photo of Bryce and him in Disney World caps. They were ten, they were best buddies, Bryce had his arm over the hunter's shoulder, and they were smiling.

The second picture frame, another silver one, the one that sits on the nightstand on her side of the bed, displays a photo of the hunter and his wife at a park. A stranger took the photo for them. His smile is real; hers is false. She was pregnant at the time with Junior, her eighth month, and she was in pain. She would go into labor that night, and Junior would be born two weeks ahead of schedule. July 2, 1999.

The third picture frame holds a photo of the hunter's mother, a slender, round-faced woman with raven hair in a red dress, and his freckle-faced father—Dada in a black suit, holding Mommy around the waist, smoking a cigarette over her shoulder. This photo, which sits in its silver frame on a shelf in the children's room, was taken before the hunter was born, a time when his parents threw loving glances at each other instead of insults. Next to this photo and its frame on this high shelf is a hideous green lamp that is unplugged because it has a short and might set the apartment on fire. Gramps made this lamp and the hunter inherited it from Dada, who inherited it from Gram.

Next to the hideous green lamp is the fourth picture

frame. This frame is golden (fake gold), and it is empty—well, not exactly empty. Professional models pose in the frame as a happy dark-haired family of four holding fishing rods in a boat on placid crystal-blue water. This empty frame will be filled with the hunter and his wife's wedding photo once she decides to accept his hand in marriage.

In this frame, between the photo of the fishing-boat family and the cardboard backing, the hunter keeps his notes.

Tonight in his notes he writes, *Mary's right. Bob is a bad daddy. I am a good daddy. Two sides of the same coin. The End.*

The hunter snaps the pencil in celebration and throws it away.

Lilies

He calls his favorite journalist and gets her answering machine.

"I'm away from my desk right now. Please leave a message at the sound of the tone."

"I wanted to speak to you, but you're not there. I wanted to tell you I'm finally happy. Did you get the flowers I left by your door? Lilies are in season."

Be Silent and Listen

It is a cool night for July.

The hottest July in ten years, but the needle barely rises above sixty. It's going to be a bad hurricane season this fall. At least eight storms will make landfall or there will be one really big storm, like Andrew from '92. A cat 4 or a cat 5. Climate change. Global warming. Blah, blah, blah. The hunter has heard this before. All he knows is that the weather's nice tonight. Hot rain doesn't fall, and he doesn't burn.

The hunter makes a call from a phone booth at a convenience store in Homestead. It is two days later. It is 10:00 p.m.

"Be silent and listen," he says.

The officer who answers tells him to wait, and he says, "Wait for what? You know who I want. Put her on. Put her on."

There is the buzz of electronic silence as the call is transferred.

"Periwinkle," the brown detective says.

"Be silent and listen," he says. "I killed the Snatcher. You can thank me now."

"Wrong, wrong, wrong. You should've given him to us," she says. "Alive. Let the courts try him. Put him in jail."

"Is that so?"

"But thank you—and I do mean this sincerely—for rescuing Jermaine."

And he tells her where on Mt. Trash-More Bob Montgomery's body can be found.

"Why the change? Why not the Everglades?"

"It was short notice. Dada did not give me time to gather my sacks. Bob will be in trash bags."

"*Dada?* You work with your father?"

"Dada's dead."

"Dead father. Okay, well. Okay," she says. She speaks to someone behind her. "What I meant was, why not the Everglades? Why the municipal dump site? Why the change?"

"Your people were at the entrance waiting for me, but I spotted them. What kind of strategy is that? You'll have to guard every entrance of the Everglades, all day, every day. Idiots," he says. "You'll never catch me like that."

"How *will* we catch you?"

"You're too stupid to catch me." He pauses. "I don't mean you personally, Detective."

He drops the phone as sirens approach.

The Periwinkle Killer

"The victim's name is Robert Franklin 'Bob' Montgomery, owner of the popular Laundromat and dry cleaning business called Round the Clock. Bob Montgomery's murder was particularly grisly, as there was extensive and brutal damage done to the face. As he has done in the past with his prior murders, the Periwinkle Killer called two days later at precisely 10:00 p.m. to inform authorities where the victim's body could be found . . ."

The Channel 7 news broadcast plays, but the hunter's concentration is disturbed by his wife's loud weeping. He finds it impossible to follow the narrative. He wants to hear what they theorize about Periwinkle.

"Eduardo, David, Carl, and Bob are the first names of the victims. The killer appears to be going through the alphabet backward. Police speculate that the name of the next victim will begin with an A. We're not sure how this information will help them find the killer, but if your name begins with A and you live in the Miami metro area, be extra cautious in the next few weeks. This is the first time Periwinkle has killed two people in the same year. He may be on what authorities call a spree . . ."

2

The hunter storms into the children's room and slams the door.

He scoffs at his wife's stubborn affection for the monster Bob and chafes at the boldness of her utter lack of it for him.

What about me? *I'm your husband. I'm the father of your children.*

When the news anchor says, "Authorities are saying there is evidence that Periwinkle's fourth victim, Robert Montgomery, owner of Round the Clock Laundromat and Dry Cleaning, may be the killer known as the Snatcher," a shrill cry comes from the other side of the door.

The hunter realizes this is his day of triumph over the pain caused by their willful and wanton sexual insolence. They got what they deserved. He should be happy. He listens more closely to her lamentations, taking pleasure in her sobs, her sudden shrieks, her blubbering, her sputtering, her half starts at saying goodbye to someone important to her. Some part deep within her has been ripped out. Some part deep within him rejoices.

He leaves the bedroom to celebrate her misery.

—She shivers in the middle of the small living room, swaying unsteadily. Hands cover her face one moment, support her loose stomach the next. Then, arms folded across her chest, she hugs herself. She says, "I can't believe he did this. It has to be a mistake. He was a nice guy. He was tender and sensitive." She looks down at her big feet. "I'm sorry. I know you don't want to hear this." She throws her head back and, trembling, screams. She says, "Bob, oh Bob, why?"

—He wants to mock her pain with mirth, but he puts his arms around her. The older kids are at his mother's. The contented cooing of Victor Ulysses, who was awakened when his father stormed into the room, comes from the door left ajar. They do not own a baby monitor. She lays her head on his shoulder, and he says, "You can keep talking if it helps. Shout. Scream. Cry out his name. I'm here for you."

"I don't want to hurt you. I won't hurt you anymore."

"He was someone you loved and it causes you pain. I understand that. You can keep talking if it makes you feel better. You're not hurting me. It doesn't hurt," he says, laughing inside.

—After she calms down, the room is quiet. He holds her, but no one speaks. Not even the baby makes a sound from the children's room.

Then she speaks. "I got stuck with you," she says. "With Junior, with this situation. I didn't love you."

"Why didn't you leave?"

"I tried to. That's why Bob—but he wasn't really an option," she says. "I thought about leaving many times, but something kept holding me back. It's funny, but I used to think about you when I was with Bob." A small laugh slips past her sobs. A strand of hair attaches itself to her lips. "It never felt like cheating until we were just lying in bed cuddling. After sex was over, I left quickly. I didn't want the intimacy, only sex, and not even that was as good as it is with you."

He holds her tight and they rock to music only they can

hear. When Victor Ulysses makes a sound in the children's room, they turn their heads, but it's a false alarm and the child soon goes back to clucking.

"We need to get that baby monitor," she says.

"Yes," he says.

There is hope. Their relationship can work.

—"I have a gift for you," she says.

"My birthday was last month," he says.

"It's not a birthday gift. It's sort of a make-up gift," she says. "Bob is dead. It's time to give it to you."

He follows her into the children's room. There is a little cabinet on the shelf next to the picture frame where their wedding photo will be. The cabinet is made for dolls. It is pink with powder-blue doors and brass knobs. It is a plaything, she had told him, something she had as a child.

That was a lie and he knew it four years ago when she had first told it.

He had been in her childhood home many times when they skipped school to fuck. There was nothing delicate and pretty like this in the double-wide trailer. Broken toys, dirty carpet, beer cans, and cigarette butts. Filthy. He always hated it. He wanted to clean it. One day, he did just that. She watched, looking bored, as he worked. After an hour of watching, she grabbed the vacuum and joined him. When the others came home, they joined in as well. Finally, the trailer was clean. It stayed that way for a week. After two weeks, it was the way it was before it had been cleaned. After three weeks, it was worse than before it had been cleaned.

The cabinet had mysteriously appeared in the children's room around the time Zoe was born. The cabinet was a gift from Bob, he was certain, but he had let her keep it because Zoe would eventually inherit it. He reasoned that a child should have something of her father's. Her blood father's. He was willing to make that concession for little brown Zoe.

Victor Ulysses gurgles contentedly. The hunter makes a funny face. He sticks out his tongue. Victor responds with an infant's clucking laughter.

His wife opens the glass door of the cabinet and takes out a small gift-wrapped box. It is a box that a wedding ring might come in.

"What is it?"

Well, it is the twenty-first century, and Mary is a modern woman. She has jobs that bring in money, more money than he earns in fact. She is free-thinking. She is in control of her feelings and sexually independent. He would love to be married to a modern woman like that. If she proposes, he will say yes, for he is a modern person too.

"Open it," she says.

He opens it.

"Where did you get this?"

"Gerardo gave it to me."

"Bryce?" That day in Tampa, Bryce his greatest champion had had his back as always, sarcastic Bryce, Bryce and his laughing eyes, Bryce in his backyard hanging from that tree, his eyes no longer laughing. Oh, Bryce. But he has to stop thinking about it. There is an opportunity before him. The silly bear on a string is in the small box.

"When Tina didn't want it, Bryce took it, but I said, 'Can I have it?' I thought it was cute. I thought you were cute too."

"I was fat."

"My dad is fat. My real dad." She picks up the silly thing and dangles it next to her face. It *is* a silly thing, the small teddy bear on a string, its shiny button eyes the same blue-gray as hers.

He seizes the opportunity and takes her hand. "Mary Eugenia Fisk, will you be my bride and make me the happiest man in the world?"

"Yes," she says. "I love you, though you're just a pizza man."

"*What?*" He fights the urge to grab her by the throat and shake her until her eyes pop out.

FIX IT

I never forgive. I never forget.
—Edgar L. Jackson

Jermaine

The 10-year-old Miami Shores boy who went missing July 7 has been returned to his family and is reportedly in good health.

In a strange twist, the missing boy was held captive by one serial killer, the Snatcher, and rescued by another, the Periwinkle Killer.

Jermaine Milkovich, the boy who was taken on his way home from school, explained his ordeal: "A car stopped next to me. The man inside asked me if I could tell him how to get to Aventura Mall. I told him I wasn't sure, but I go there all the time with my mom and dad. He got out of the car with a map and said, 'Show me where you think it is on the map.' I told him I don't know how to read a map real good, and he grabbed me and everything got all foggy."

Jermaine Milkovich is slowly returning to a normal life after his harrowing encounter with the notorious Snatcher who had held South Florida in a grip of fear for more than a decade.

Authorities believe there may be a connection between the Snatcher and the Periwinkle Killer. The prominent use of flowers in both their rituals is hard to ignore. But there is no evidence that the Periwinkle Killer and the Snatcher worked together as a "killing team," as some suggest.

Jermaine Milkovich, the Snatcher's rescued victim,

said of Periwinkle, "He was a nice man. He gave me water to drink and spaghetti to eat. He wanted to get me back home, he said. I liked him. I hope he gives himself up so everyone can see that he is nice."

Authorities say Periwinkle, who has already struck twice this month, is on what they are calling a spree. One thing we can say with a relative amount of certainty is that no child will be taken on Periwinkle's spree. He seems to have some sort of emotional connection to children.

Periwinkle told police in his ritual 10:00 p.m. phone call two days after he murdered the Snatcher that he does not prey on children. "I exterminate rats," he reportedly said, by which the police presume he meant people who hurt children, like two of his victims.

—Heidi Renoir-Smith, *Miami Herald*

Unknown Serial Killer

The skeletal remains of a man unearthed last week, as construction crews were demolishing the parking lot to expand the shopping center at Main Street in Miami Lakes, have been identified as Rutledge King.

King, who was so long buried that his clothes had disintegrated into layers of fine powder and dust, was last seen in June of 1981.

The FBI believes there may be a connection between Rutledge King and a woman whose body was discovered in March of last year.

The woman, who was identified as Mary Mercedes, had had her head, arms, and legs removed from her torso with surgical precision. Like King, who was similarly dissected, Mercedes's body parts were buried in separate holes. Mary Mercedes was last seen alive in January of 1982.

Rutledge King was a research engineer for ITTM Tech Labs with mob ties. In 1981, King lived in a home with a large mortgage, drove an expensive luxury car, and was rumored to have relationships with multiple women.

To finance his lifestyle, King borrowed money from fringe criminal elements associated with the Ferragamo crime family. He paid them back, the FBI believes, by selling phenobarbital to his coworkers.

According to FBI records, King had been under

surveillance but disappeared before he could be arrested. The FBI report notes that when they entered King's home, the last place he was seen, it was "clean to the point of immaculate."

Police records from 1981–82 indicate that Mercedes was a prostitute who went by the street name "Lord'da Mercy." The territory she worked was 79th Street and Biscayne Boulevard. Her pimp and small-time record producer, Mark "Sugar" Johnson, allegedly owed money to a loan shark with ties to the Ferragamo family.

The FBI suspects both King and Mercedes were killed by the notorious Ferragamo enforcer Tony "Scarface" Fava, but they cannot explain why the severed limbs were arranged like da Vinci's Vitruvian Man.

—Heidi Renoir-Smith, *Miami Herald*

Charlemagne

Edgar L. Jackson was fired from his job as a test engineer at McManus Systems, a company that designed computer technologies for NASA.

He was fired for drunkenness.

After that, he worked for ITTM Tech Labs as a systems manager until he was fired from that job for drunkenness. Because of his addiction to alcohol, he was fired from three more engineering jobs. Then he took a position with Briggs Brothers Construction. He was licensed to operate a truck-mounted augur and he knew his way around tools from working with his father, who was a stonemason. It seemed a good fit, but the drinking. Before he could be fired from his construction job, he found help in the Twelve Steps of Alcoholics Anonymous:

> *Step 1. We admitted we were powerless over alcohol and that our lives had become unmanageable.*
> *Step 2. We came to believe that a Power greater than ourselves could restore us to sanity.*
> *Step 3. We made a decision to turn our lives over to the care of God as we understood Him to be.*
> *Step 4. We made a searching and fearless inventory of ourselves.*
> *Step 5. We admitted to God, to ourselves, and to one other human being the exact nature of our wrongs.*

On Step 5, Edgar L. Jackson disappeared Charlie.

—Charlemagne Renoir, "Charlie" for short, was a childhood friend and drinking buddy of Edgar L. Jackson's. Behind Edgar's back, Charlie had slept with his wife. She confessed to her husband, who confronted Charlie.

Charlie apologized profusely and blamed it on his addiction.

"When I drink, I don't know what I'm doing. I can't control myself."

"So, you just bang my wife."

"It was just the one time. I'm sorry, I don't know what else to say. We go way back. We, me and you—that's why I confessed."

"*She* confessed."

"I didn't deny it."

"Makes me feel much better that you didn't deny it."

"I could've denied it, but I didn't." Charlie wagged a finger. It was a habit of his when he was getting annoyed. He did wrong, but he felt he was being persecuted. Edgar was persecuting him. "What else can I do?" he said, wagging that finger. "What else can I do?"

—"*Step 5. Admit to one other human being the exact nature of your wrongs,*" Edgar said to his best friend Charlie.

"*You* admit your wrongs," Charlie fired back. "Again, I tell you that I'm sorry. Want me to say it again? I'm sorry. The details are private and to you they would be terrible. I'm sorry, but are you a pervert? You're my friend, not a cuck."

The pool table took up most of the space in Charlie's home, which was a single-wide trailer in the Princely Manor Trailer Park in Miami Lakes since his wife had left him and taken his three kids and their house a year earlier. The smell was cheap perfume from the hooker who had left before Edgar arrived, and urine because Charlie did not lift the toilet seat, nor clean it either, and beer because Charlie had backslid. He was drinking again. He had not only betrayed Edgar, he had betrayed himself.

Edgar had brought a small slate-gray toolbox with him, the kind you carry in your hand. He set it on the pool table.

Edgar and Charlie were alone in the trailer.

—July 25, 1982, was the fourth Sunday in the month.

It was hot in the trailer. Outside the grimy window, Edgar could see a half-built on-ramp that half led to the Palmetto Expressway before it came to a sloping incompletion, like a ramp built for skateboard daredevil jumps, except that you'd jump off into the unforgiving traffic of the expressway.

When are they going to finish the on-ramp? Edgar wondered. *They've been working on it for a year. Maybe Charlie can be buried there.*

Charlie was fit, but not a big man. The ground the half-built ramp was built on could sustain a hole deep enough to hold Charlie.

Closer to home, Briggs Brothers Construction was breaking ground for the new mall that would put the township of Palmetto Cove on par with its big sisters, Hialeah and Miami Lakes. At the Palmetto Cove Fashion Mall there would be a JCPenney, a multiplex movie theater, a Thom McAn shoe store, a food court, a Sam Goody record store, and so on like that.

A hole deep enough to hold Charlie could be dug there.

Then again, there was the cow pasture on the east side of I-75 where he walked at night when the voices claimed him. He loved his wife, but the voices did not. They accused her of being disloyal. He disagreed. He explained to them that at sixteen he had kissed her for the first time on the playground that used to be here. There were other girls, true. For her, there were other guys, but he got over it—the voices did not. He loved his wife, his soul mate. On this playground, he proposed to her the first time, and the second, and the third. A hole deep enough to hold Charlie could be dug in the cow pasture.

He couldn't decide which of the three sites to use, and the voices in his head were of no help.

They had never done a best friend before. They were loud and chattering excitedly. In their enthusiasm to get it done, they were as confused as he was. Gram was the loudest of the voices, but all he could make out was her screeching: *Fix it!*

—Edgar was a fix-it man, so Charlie was not surprised that he had brought the mini toolbox. Edgar and his tools. He was always fixing things for his friends.

Whatever he was working on was a one-man job or he would've asked Charlie to assist him. Charlie was not as good with tools as Edgar was, but he was good at assisting. He was the extra muscle for heavy lifting, the sidekick who knew all the best jokes. This was a key to their friendship that went all the way back to childhood.

Edgar the hard worker. Charlie the kidder.

—"It's a hoax. It doesn't work. I completed all twelve steps and I still need to drink," Charlie said. "Making amends is what did it. Steps 8 and 9 screwed me over with my wife. I think it's what led to—you know. I think it led to that."

"But you cheated Step 5. You never admitted the exact nature of your wrongs to God and to someone else. I'm here. Admit the exact nature of your wrongs to me."

Charlie turned on him. He wagged the finger. "Admit to me the exact nature of *your* wrongs, Edgar, like I give a damn."

"Okay. I've got five."

"Go ahead. Admit them."

Edgar went over to the slate-gray toolbox and calmly opened it. "One, I kill people, Charlie." There were two wrenches and a ball-peen hammer in the toolbox. Edgar took out the ball-peen hammer, and turned to Charlie. "I kill whores mostly, and friends who sleep with my wife."

Charlie jumped from his chair.

Moving with the swiftness and agility of a cornered cat, he made it past Edgar, who was the bigger man. He made it to the door. Before he could make it through the door, Edgar struck his head with the hammer.

—When Charlie regained consciousness, Edgar admitted to him the rest of his five wrongs, his voice as emotionless as the ball-peen hammer in his hand.

"Two, I have dark thoughts about killing you, Charlie. Three, the dark thoughts have been telling me to kill you since ninth grade when you copied my paper and told Mrs. Hanna that it was me who copied yours when she asked us why our papers were identical. Four, the dark thoughts warned me you were a false friend. I loved you, so I ignored them. But sleeping with my wife is the final straw. Five, I'm going to pound your head to mush with this ball-peen hammer."

Charlie's skull was fissured from the blow. The pain was excruciating and his eyes could not focus. No plea for mercy was possible with the filthy dish towel in his mouth. He could not gesture with his hands, which were tied together behind his back and bound to the chair with an extension cord.

Edgar rested a hand on Charlie's shoulder like someone lending comfort to a friend. "You should thank me. It's better than what the dark thoughts are telling me to do. They're telling me to dig a hole and put you in it while alive."

The dish towel in Charlie's mouth tasted like peanut butter and ass. After sex with the prostitute, he had wiped with this dish towel. Yesterday when the kids came over, they had made peanut butter and jelly sandwiches on Wonder Bread. They had had a lot of fun, but he neglected to clean up. Didn't want to, really. His ex called him a slob. He was, but the kids loved him for it. Charlie shook his fissured head desperately.

"You're my friend, so I'll make a deal with you." Edgar walked over to the radio and turned it on. He twisted the dial until he heard the bass riff of Michael Jackson's "Working Day and Night." He turned the volume all the way up so the neighbors wouldn't hear Charlie's screams. "If you thank me for beating you to death with the hammer, I won't bury you while you're still alive."

Edgar removed the dish towel from Charlie's mouth so that he could hear his answer over the traffic on the Palmetto Expressway and the funky bass riff of the Michael Jackson song. Charlie wanted to rub his eyes, but he couldn't. They were wet with tears and burned when he blinked. They could not focus.

"Why?" Charlie said. "Why?"

"I told you why. Stop asking why."

"But why?" Charlie had fallen on his face after the hammer blow to the head. His lips had burst on his teeth and the blood in his mouth tasted like copper. "Oh, please don't kill me, Edgar. Please don't kill me. My children, Claire, Heidi, and Bobby. They're your godchildren. I did wrong, I hurt you, I betrayed you, but for their sake, oh please don't kill me."

"Now, Charlie, that's not one of your choices," Edgar admonished patiently as to a child. "Listen carefully. Thank me for beating you to death with the hammer, or I'll stuff the towel back in your mouth, dig a hole, and put you in it."

"But Edgar, oh Edgar, please Edgar," Charlie pleaded.

Edgar slapped his palm with the hammer. "Put you in it while *alive*."

At last, Charlie's eyes were able to focus. Edgar held the dish towel in his right hand and the ball-peen hammer in his left. "No!" Charlie said, surging against his bonds. The chair rattled, tilted, and almost tipped over. He couldn't break free.

Edgar's face was impassive.

Charlie wept at the hopelessness of his situation. A sloppy mess of tears and snot, he finally said, "Thank you for beating me to death with the hammer."

And Edgar beat him to death with the hammer.

Then he took him to the pasture on the east side of I-75, where the cows watched in silence as he dug a hole and put Charlie in it.

The Hideous Lamp

Perhaps pigs can fly
Perhaps a camel can pass through a needle's eye
Perhaps the governor will stay my execution
Perhaps there are snowballs in hell
—Etched into Dada's cell wall at the Florida State Prison
at Starke

When Dada was caught with another woman, Mommy
scolded him angrily.

"You hypocrite—always throwing in my face what I did
with Charlie. Wherever he went, I wish I was there with him.
But you and this woman—the mother of your son's best
friend."

"Look who's talking."

"Is Gerardo yours?"

"Look who's talking." Dada put his hands over his ears.
"Look who's talking."

This was Poe's favorite argument of theirs. When this argument came, his ears perked up, collecting the clues Mommy
would list. Dada and Gerardo's mom were girlfriend and
boyfriend in high school. Gerardo's mom was pregnant when
she said her vows to Gerardo's father. *What vows and what
is a vow?* Was Bryce his actual brother?

But this time the argument was different somehow.

"Go be with your black tramp. I hope her husband beats
your ass. I hope he kills you," she said.

"Look who's talk—"

Mommy slapped his face. "Get out."

Dada flinched, but Poe was unmoved. She had said that one before.

"We're finished," Mommy said.

She had never said *that* before.

Dada retreated to the guest room to heal from the injuries both psychic and physical that she had inflicted. Poe quietly followed him in. Dada was dabbing at his eyes with a handkerchief. "I really messed up this time. Mommy wants me to leave home."

"But why, Dada?"

"Mommy wants me to go. Maybe forever."

"Forever? But why, Dada?"

Dada spread his arms and Poe went to him and was sheltered in them. "One thing you can depend on," Dada said, "is that I love you. And I'll always be here for you."

Dada explained about divorce and why it was wrong and how it would hurt like you wouldn't believe. That's why Poe should be strong, even though he himself couldn't be. He was weak. So weak.

"Don't leave, Dada. What about me?"

As the clock in the belly of the hideous green lamp that sat on the table next to the small twin bed steadily ticked, Dada explained that he loved Poe, and Mommy, and their little family so much he could just die.

Tick-tock. Tick-tock.

The hideous lamp had a gaping green hole at the top. Was the hole the mouth of a large toad? Would a tongue suddenly whip out and pull you in? Was it a place to put flowers? Would a flower suddenly sprout? Was it a toad trying to be a flowerpot? Was it a flowerpot trying to be a toad? Poe had always wondered as he hid here in this room when they fought, and they fought a lot. Not just about Gerardo, but other stuff. Gram hated her, said Mommy was not good enough for Dada, who was educated and smart, said Mommy was trash, said she came from the other side of the tracks. Where was the other side of the tracks? Sometimes Poe wanted to be that hideous, headless, big-mouth toad. Sometimes, like the toad, he wanted to be a flowerpot. Anything was better than being himself, stuck in the middle of two people he loved, being pulled on hard from both sides when they fought.

The hideous lamp was constructed of wrought iron. With its bloated belly, it weighed as much as a second grader, and was about as tall. It had two spindly iron legs. There was no torso—iron arms grew out of the bloated belly. There was no lampshade and no place to put one. A bare bulb sat exposed on a crossbar that spanned the gaping mouth. Turn on the lamp and the bulb would explode due to the faulty wiring.

The only part of the lamp that worked was the windup clock, which ticked loudly but kept perfect time.

Tick-tock. Tick-tock.

The clock face was hidden under the belly of the deformed creature. To check the time, you had to tilt the heavy, wrought-iron thing.

Mommy said whoever made the lamp was either drunk or blind. She wouldn't have it in their bedroom, so it was kept in this room for houseguests to ponder.

Tick-tock. Tick-tock.

Dada wouldn't part with it. First of all, he knew the artist who made it. Gramps, his father. He kept it for sentimental reasons. Secondly, Gram, his mother, had beaten an intruder to death with the lamp, which she had held by the legs and swung like a baseball bat. The intruder's head had met the lamp seventeen times until it was more pulp than bone. Some say the story was an exaggeration, that no woman possessed such strength, that maybe the intruder fell and hit his head on the lamp, or that if Gram did hit him with it she only hit him once, certainly no more than twice, but Dada had been in the room that night and kept count while she did it.

Whack.

Fifteen.

Whack.

Sixteen.

Whack.

Seventeen.

Some say the dead man was not an intruder, but Gram's lover. Dada was often alone in the house with Gram and knew that that was true too, but kept it secret from his father. Gram told him not to tell because it would break up the family. A good boy is good at keeping secrets. And Dada was a good boy.

"Gram told me what to do if I can't keep my family together." He grabbed the heavy lamp by one of its spindly iron legs. "She told me to smash your head. Smash Mommy's head. Then slit my own throat, and we'll all be together in heaven."

Poe pushed away, tried to run. Dada caught him with his free hand.

Gram screeched: *Fix it! Fix it!*

Poe twisted and squirmed, hit his father, kicked his father.

"Stop moving around so much, you little bastard," Dada said. "Try to understand."

Poe continued to struggle, and Dada held him fast. He could see in Poe's eyes that he was about to scream. He released the lamp and put his hand over Poe's mouth before he could scream.

Dada appealed to his son: "I'll kill Mommy too and she'll be in heaven with us."

Poe bit into Dada's hand. He didn't want to die.

Without flinching, Dada said, "Don't fight it, Poe."

Gram screeched: *Fix it! Fix it!*

Mommy appeared at the door.

"What are you doing, Edgar?"

Dada couldn't move his hand from Poe's mouth. Poe's teeth were clenched so hard they had become sticky with blood, but Mommy couldn't see the blood squirting through Dada's fingers because Dada's wide back blocked it all.

Gram screeched: *Hit the slut with the lamp! Bash her brains out! Fix it!*

—"What are you doing to him, Edgar?" Mommy asked.

"I'm telling him a secret."

Poe unclenched his teeth and wrenched away from Dada's hand. Now he could run. He could scream. He could tell Mommy that Dada was going to kill them all, but he didn't. He just waited. He didn't want to break up a family.

Mommy said, "Keep him out of this."

"If you're going to leave me, he'll know soon enough."

"He's a child."

"I want him to understand," Dada said. "Mothers always turn the children against their fathers, that's what."

As his father's warm blood swirled in his mouth, Poe recalled what all the kids of divorced parents at school said. They loved their dad, but Mommy kept him away. They only got to see him on weekends. When the fun got really good, it would suddenly end and they had to go back home. Then Mommy would ask questions that they were too embarrassed to answer because he was their dad and he was fun. *Did he buy you a bed yet or do you still sleep on that stupid blow-up mattress? Does he give you just cereal for breakfast? How many times did you guys eat at Burger King? Does his girlfriend sleep over?*

"Turn him against you? What makes you think I would do that? I wouldn't do that. He worships you," Mommy said.

"That's what you say now," Dada said.

Mommy threw up her hands and walked out of the room. "To hell with you. Tell him what you want," she could be heard saying outside the room.

"You bet I will," Dada said over his shoulder to the sound of Mommy's footsteps retreating down the hallway to the kitchen. He turned to Poe. "It's a lie. She never married me. We're not married."

—"She wouldn't do it. She's not my wife. We didn't want to shame you, thinking your mom was not virtuous."

Mommy shouted from the kitchen: "So why are you telling him *now*? Now you're shaming him because I tell you to leave. We could've made up, you know. We could've worked on it. It's not like I don't still love you." In the kitchen something banged. It sounded like the fry pan hitting the stove top. "You're a drunk! Get out!" A crash. The coffee maker landing on the ground maybe. "Not virtuous? That's a man's word for a woman who has the same feelings men have. Like you and your colored whore. What about that, huh?" She was loud and angry, but there were tears in her voice too.

Poe didn't know what *virtuous* meant, he didn't know what *whore* meant, but he wasn't afraid anymore. He pulled Dada's hand onto his head. "Kill me, Dada. Dead together in heaven is better than divorce."

Poe's words shocked Dada. Poe was his legacy. He removed his hand from Poe's head. "Not yet," he said. Poe was his legacy, but the affair—after all these years it still drove him crazy. Did he hate Charlemagne that much? He loved his wife. He loved Poe. He wouldn't kill them for Charlemagne's sin.

Dada's eyes were bloodshot from tears. He reached behind his neck, unclasped the gold chain he always wore, and hung it around Poe's neck. "This is for you."

"For me, Dada?" Poe had always liked Dada's chain. He felt so grown up wearing it. He looked just like Dada wearing it.

"And don't lose the lamp. You may need it one day." Dada tapped the hideous, ticking, wrought-iron thing. "Who knows what kind of bitch you're going to marry."

"What's a *bitch*, Dada?"

Dada pinched his nose playfully and hugged him. Then he went out and killed a stranger he met in a bar.

Unlike the others, this murder was impulsive. Three men held him down until the police arrived. In court, he was sentenced to thirty years to life. In prison, he was killed by his cellmate over a cigarette.

—When Poe saw him again, Dada was in a pine box. His eyes were closed above a peaceful, freckle-faced smile.

The prison chaplain said a brief prayer, and Dada's coffin was lowered into the ground by silent, bare-chested brown men using shovels, wood planks, and strong rope.

The Babysitter

There was a girl.

When he said the N-word, she corrected him.

"Then what can I call them?"

"Call them people."

"But what color people?"

"Just don't call them that word. It's hurtful."

"I don't want to hurt anybody," said the boy. "Can I call them Negroes?"

"I don't think they want to be called that anymore."

"What about *colored*? My mom calls them colored."

"I don't think they want to be called colored anymore either."

"Can I call them black?"

"Yes. That would be acceptable."

"What about brown?"

"Brown? Why brown?"

"I got a good look at them. They're brown, not black," he said.

"Did you get a good look at all of them?" she said.

He tapped his lips with a forefinger and squinted, the gesture he made when suspicious. She was always trying to trick him. "No, not all of them," he said, laughing.

"Take a good look at me," she said.

He took a good look at her. Oh boy, did he take a good look. He always looked at her as much as he could—at her pink face, at her dark hair that fell in soft curls that he wanted to touch with his fingers. "Okay. I took a good look at you," he said, smiling inside because of the secret behind his words.

The girl said, "My dad's grandfather was black. He was French Creole. What does that make me, black?"

She couldn't be black. She was pretty, and he wanted to play with her soft hair. He had a crush on her. She was his babysitter. Of course he was in love with her. That was the secret he held inside.

"No, it does not make you black," said the boy. "It makes you brown."

"Brown," she said. "You're so cute."

"I'm cute?" he said. "I'm fat and everybody says I'm ugly."

"Don't listen to anyone who says you're ugly. You're cute. Cute times a hundred," she said to the boy who would grow up to become the hunter.

"You're cute too," the boy who would grow up to become the hunter said to his babysitter. "Cute times a thousand!"

COMING UNRAVELED

I Dream of Dada

In dreams he can see his father no matter where he stands—before him, behind him, by his side.

Kill the bitch, Dada says. *Bash her head in.*

The hunter's eyes snap open.

She's still there, resting against him, his wife. He can't decide how he feels about her anymore. The images of her and Bob play in his head again, over and over like a film loop. But even worse: *You're just a pizza man,* she had said.

He enters the room where the children sleep and the hideous lamp is kept. They brought it with them when they moved and keep it on the high bureau where the kids can't reach. Like Mommy, the hunter's wife hates it. Like Mommy, the hunter's wife is not virtuous. Like Mommy, she comes from the other side of the tracks.

Dada said, *One day you might need the lamp.*

Little Zoe sleeps on her back, her smooth, brown head against the soft feather pillow, her mouth slightly open. Her face tightens as though she is disturbed at the thought of her father leaning over her contemplating smashing her brown head with the hideous lamp.

Zoe's eyes open. She smiles at him, says, "I love you, Daddy," and her eyes close once more. He reaches for her in her bed.

Behind him there is movement, and he swings his arm.

"Be careful. You almost hit me," his wife says. She takes his empty hand and together they watch their children sleep.

After a while she says, "Let's go back to bed. You coming?"

He says, "I'm horny."

"Well, if we're careful, there are things we can do," she says, and purses her lips for a kiss.

He touches her panties.

"That's what you want? I just had a baby. I can hardly walk." She laughs because she thinks it is a joke.

He is suddenly angry.

Then she becomes angry.

But he's still aroused. "Then use your hand."

"I will not."

"Oh, I see. You fucked Bob, but you won't fuck me," he says. "You fucked a child murderer."

"I didn't know he was a child murderer."

"He would've killed Zoe if he had lived."

"I said I did not know!"

"You fucked him."

"Fuck you!"

"Yes. Fuck me!"

She grabs him by the crotch and leads him into their bedroom, where she uses her hand. She is angry and disgusted by it. When she notices the strain on his part to enjoy it, her anger dissolves and her disgust turns into fear.

Separate and apart on most things are they, but on this they agree: no matter how much it arouses you, you must not kill your family.

2

He wakes up in an unpleasant mood.

He ignores his children's spirited calls for breakfast. When his wife jokingly complains that someone has to feed them, he rolls over and faces the wall. He tells her, "Go away."

"Come on, Poe, they love your French toast," she says, but he is unresponsive.

Because of last night, she says nothing more. She leaves him and goes to feed their brood.

He doesn't know what he might do if he goes to make breakfast. He doesn't know what he might do if he sees them. *Please, God, keep me from hurting them.*

3

He hears the fuss as they leave for church. He hears the fuss as they return. No one disturbs him and he doesn't come out of the bedroom until three in the afternoon.

The clothes need to be washed and folded, the floor swept, the garbage taken down to the incinerator. He sits in the settee in his bathrobe staring at the blank TV screen. His wife turns it on. A silly Old Spice commercial plays on the screen.

"What do you want to watch?" she says.

"Doesn't matter. Leave it there," he says.

"Doesn't matter?" she says.

"Okay. I'll get out of your way."

"You're not in my way."

"I'm getting out of here. It's too hot," he says.

He takes off his robe and stands naked in the middle of the living room. The thought of killing them arouses him. The children giggle.

"Daddy is a muscle man," Junior says.

"Make a muscle, Daddy," Zoe says.

His wife jumps between him and the children. "Put some clothes on!"

He goes into the bedroom. Ten minutes later, he reappears in his pizza T-shirt and jeans.

"Thomas," he says to his wife. "The next baby's name will be Thomas if it's a boy."

She stands there looking at him, breathing hard, her eyes narrowed to pinpoints.

"What are you looking at? Stop looking at me," he says. "I'm just a pizza man, huh?" He puts on his cap and tips the bill.

"Wait," she says.

He walks out of the apartment and slams the door.

4

Tonight, he goes on no deliveries. He counts the receipts and helps with the phones, but he makes mistakes. He can't add. He can't subtract. He can't concentrate, so he goes in the back by the ovens and makes the pizzas. After a half dozen tosses that land on the floor, he puts one of the others in charge. In the office, he sits at the desk and counts down. Five hours, four, three, two, one, and then it is midnight. There is a driver, Kathy, a slender girl with big eyes who has flirted with him in the past. She enters the office. His experience with girls is limited. One who stole his heart. One who bore his children. And his favorite journalist who covers his deeds accurately and without prejudice.

Kathy lingers. Is she communicating her feelings as she inquires about next week's schedule? She is overly familiar, flirtatious even, twisting and untwisting a lock of blond hair that falls behind her left ear. If he wanted to, he might be able to persuade Kathy to have a Coke with him after everyone has left. He is more nervous than aroused. He doesn't ask her, and she leaves his office. He watches them close the store without helping, watches them get into their cars, and then he is alone.

—He calls his favorite journalist.

"I'm away from my desk right now. Please leave a message at the sound of the tone."

"I just wanted to talk, but I guess you're away from your desk. For the love of God, pick up."

His favorite journalist picks up. "It's late. What time is it?" she says.

"Did you get the pizza I left outside your door?"

"I threw it away," she says.

"Someone is going to die tonight."

"Call a suicide hotline."

"That's not funny."

"I'll call them for you," she says.

"Not me. I'm not going to kill myself."

"I didn't think so. Good night."

"Sleep well, Heidi Renoir-Smith," he says. "Sleep well."

—After that, he calls his wife.

"Poe? What's wrong?"

"Go into the kids' room," he says. "Do it now!"

There is the mousy noise of feet shuffling across the uncarpeted floor in her favorite slippers as she enters their room. The yawning of the door hinges, the ceiling fan squeaking as it spins, stirring hot air around the room, the shallow huffing breaths of a woman who has recently given birth as she obediently follows his commands—the familiar sounds of home.

"Put the phone by Junior's face. I want to hear him breathe."

She does.

"Oh, Poe."

"Put the phone by Xavier's face and then by Victor's."

She does.

"Oh, Poe. What's happening?"

"Put the phone by Zoe Montgomery's brown face."

She says, "Is that what it's about? Zoe?"

"She's my daughter, and I want to hear her breathe. Put the damned phone by her face."

After she does, he says, "Why didn't you marry me before, when I asked?"

"I didn't love you."

"You loved Bob."

"I never loved Bob," she says.

"You said you did," he says.

"Please come home, baby."

"You said I'm just a pizza man. To hell with you!" He rips the phone from the wall. "I don't hear talking dogs. I'm not a killer clown. I'm just a pizza man, but God help me, I fix it."

He drops into the chair at the table where the schedule is made and works on next week's schedule. He gives Kathy Saturday off, which is what she was sniffing around for. When the schedule is completed, he thumbtacks it to the corkboard wall.

He goes in the storeroom at the back of the restaurant where he keeps a party shirt and dress pants. He removes the pizza uniform and puts the party clothes on. He comes out and inspects the store one final time. Everything is clean. Everything is wiped down and lemony fresh.

He opens the door and steps out into the night.

Arne

At 1:07 a.m., the hunter arrives at Big Daddy Hennigan's Pub.

The room is dark and cool. It smells of alcohol and cigarette smoke. A handful of late-night drinkers are at the bar. Earlier that evening there had been a live musical performance of some kind, and a drum set and a microphone on a microphone stand are still set up in a corner, but now recorded jazz music flows from hidden speakers. A tenor saxophone sails slowly on a soft piano sea.

"One beer. One whiskey," the hunter says to the barkeep, a man in a dirty white shirt with a wet face like a weeping bulldog. After paying with a five and two crumpled singles, he takes a seat in the back where the lights have been dimmed and a few of the tables have chairs stacked on them.

He washes his mouth with the whiskey and spits it on his shirt to give it that drunk smell. He waits an hour before moving up to the bar to pick a fight with the dead man in the Miami Dolphins cap. He carries the stein of beer, which he has not touched.

". . . yer mother-frigging right I frigging said the frigging Dolphins are gonna do it this year. Somebody's gotta take out these Patriots," the dead man in the Dolphins cap says.

"Not this year. Colts all the way," the hunter says.

"Dolphins. We got a seriously revamped defense. We're building a team."

"Colts. We already have a team."

"Dolphins," the dead man says, getting angrier.

The hunter throws the beer in the dead man's face. "Colts," the hunter says.

The dead man in the Dolphins cap hits back, jamming the heel of his hand into the hunter's mouth, pushing the lips against the teeth. The hunter grabs him by the collar and they roll off their stools and onto the floor with a loud crash. Grunting, they punch each other until the bartender and bouncer pull them apart.

"Don't make me have to call the cops," the bartender warns.

The dead man in the Dolphins cap flips open his badge wallet. "I *am* a cop," says Thick Face, the cop.

The bartender says to Thick Face, "Well, you oughta know better."

"Yeah, yeah," Thick Face says, slurring. He has a tricky time replacing the badge wallet in the back pocket of his pants.

"Yeah. Yeah," the hunter says, slurring, though he is completely sober. He's not a drinker. He has come here to hunt.

He offers his hand, and Thick Face says, "Yeah. Why not?" and shakes it.

The hunter pays for Thick Face's drink. Their conversation is rich and this surprises him. He didn't think he could like a dead man. Maybe Thick Face truly didn't know it was a kid, as he said in the news. It was dark. On the other hand, Heidi Renoir-Smith's article cast some doubt on his version of the story. But Thick Face is very likable, and after an hour, the hunter calls it off. Thick Face will live.

They laugh together until the hunter asks: "Have you heard what they're doing about that Bob Montgomery guy?"

"About who?"

"The last guy Periwinkle killed."

"What about him?"

"There were skeletons in Bob Montgomery's closet too."

"Yeah, ain't that something?" Though drunk, Thick Face knows he is not to engage in discussions about this with anyone outside of law enforcement until they make sense of what went down, but the hunter has a familiar face. Probably works in a different district. Probably met him at a union meeting. Thick Face says in a lowered voice, "Friggin' Snatcher versus Periwinkle. Ain't that something?"

"Yeah, that is something," the hunter says. "But are they any closer to catching Periwinkle?"

"Maybe Snatcher worked with Periwinkle."

"What?" the hunter says. "Periwinkle doesn't kill kids."

"They're ying and yang, my friend."

"*Yin* and yang," the hunter corrects. "Periwinkle does not kill kids."

"Like ying and yang. Two sides of the same coin. One goes after the kids, the other goes after the grown-ups. Ain't that something?" A bleary-eyed Thick Face takes a swallow of the hunter's fourth free drink and sets the glass down carefully so that none of its contents will spill. "Don't care what the bigwigs say, some of us have this theory. We thought it had something to do with Hispanics until he got to Carl Graham. Why a white guy? Then he got Montgomery, and we saw the light. The first two, the spics, were caramel-colored. And then Graham. Up close, no. On his driver license, no. But from a distance, maybe in the dark, with his ruddy complexion, yes. The children, all of them, same complexion. They are hate crimes. One does the fathers, one does the kids. Those two monsters were trying to do some good."

"Good?"

"They were trying to wipe out the black race."

The hunter flinches.

"I'm joking. You can take a joke, right?" Thick Face says.

A new song plays. A jazz trumpet sails slowly on the soft piano sea.

The hunter takes a pretend sip of the beer that he is no longer drinking. "I have a theory too," he says into Thick Face's red-veined eyes. "The monsters aren't connected at all. The Snatcher made a mistake and snatched from the wrong guy, a killer worse than himself. It's got nothing to do with race."

"But the victims are all n—"

"Brown," says the hunter, cutting him off. "Montgomery and the victims were all brown."

"Brown. I see." The bouncer sitting at the end of the bar is a black man, and Thick Face thinks he understands. With a nod, he raises his shot glass to the bouncer, who ignores him. He turns back to the hunter. "You contradict yourself. It adds up to race, and you say it's not about race. What kind of crazy theory is that?"

"I'm saying maybe Periwinkle's victims aren't so random."

"Right," Thick Face says. "There's the alphabet thing."

"There's that."

"He's on *A* now, right?"

The hunter nods.

"What a coincidence. I'm Arne."

"Yes," says the hunter. "Arne Duncan."

"Next one could be me, huh?"

"If you're good, you have nothing to worry about, Arne," the hunter says, getting used to the taste of the word *Arne* in his mouth. "Periwinkle only kills rats. The first rat beat his wife so bad she lost a child. The second was an adulterer. Adultery hurts marriages. Broken marriages hurt children. Periwinkle killed the rat. Problem solved."

Thick Face sips his drink. "Is that so?"

"That is so."

"And you know all this *how?*"

"I do my research, Arne," the hunter says. He lifts the glass of beer that he is not drinking, peers over the top of it at Thick Face, taking the measure of the man. Close to six feet, a little over two hundred pounds, and obese according to the charts. He sets the glass back on the napkin and continues his narrative: "The third was a pedophile, and we know what that means. The fourth was Montgomery. The fifth may be a cop. Are you a good cop, Arne?"

The trumpet sailing slowly on a soft piano sea is joined by a frenetically flitting flute. Then comes the drum solo. Brash. Bold. The drummer beats an impetuous rhythm. The soft piano sea grows turbulent. So cool, man. So cool.

"I'm a good cop," Thick Face says.

"Are you sure? I do my research, Arne," the hunter reminds. "The first time we met, I looked you up."

"We've met before. I thought so!"

"You were involved in that little incident—"

"Hey now. What is this?"

"The newspaper said he was only thirteen—"

"They got it all wrong."

"You shot a child."

"I'm a good cop! It was dark. I tried to help him."

"After you shot him."

"Hey now." Thick Face studies the hunter with rheumy eyes. "What department did you say you worked for?"

"Didn't say I was a cop, Arne."

Behind the cash register, the bartender polishes a wineglass with a dish towel. The bouncer, balanced on his stool at the end of the bar, half listens as a gray-haired man in a dark guayabera tells him a joke. The gray-haired jokester nurses a whiskey, the bouncer sips from a glass of water, eyes watchful.

The hunter slips a stick of peppermint gum in his mouth. "What I said was, Periwinkle kills rats. He doesn't hurt kids."

"Yes," Thick Face says. "We should all be like Periwinkle. We should help the kids." And just like that, Thick Face is back to being delightfully high. He lifts the shot glass to his mouth, frowns when he finds it empty, sets it back on the bar, scoops a handful of nuts from a silver tray between them, and stuffs them in his mouth. He raises the empty glass and speaks between munches. "Here's to Periwinkle, savior of brown children!"

"Here, here," says the hunter without raising his glass. "We've all got a little Periwinkle in us."

At the end of the night, a new song plays. A trombone sails slowly on a soft piano sea. Thick Face and the hunter lean against each other like old friends and stumble out of Big Daddy Hennigan's Pub. Seventeen minutes later, Thick Face is dumped in an alley without his cap, shirt, gun, or his thick head. Periwinkles float in a pool of red around the dead man's headless torso.

Tag

The hunter's wife dabs at her eyes with sheets of toilet paper, but the tears continue to flow. *Trash*, Poe would say. *Use tissue.* She would respond, *Toilet paper* is *tissue paper, asshole.* He would say, *But you're not supposed to use it on your face unless you're trash.* And she would say, *Well, you should use it on your face, because you're an asshole, asshole.* That's the way they fight. Back and forth like children playing tag. Then somehow they end up in bed. But tonight. What's wrong with Poe tonight?

She agreed to marry him like he's wanted from the day Junior was born. She thought accepting his proposal would make him happy. But last night in the children's room, there was another fight about Bob. Today he stormed out. A few hours later, he made that strange call.

He wanted to hear his children breathe.

There are things about him that even she does not understand after four kids and half a decade of living together.

The brutal way he defended her in high school. The beating he gave Chucho. The beating he gave Bob. The boy whose hands he broke over a fake gold chain. She used to take comfort in knowing he would never harm her or the kids. But there is something dangerous lurking in him, something he tries hard to suppress. Last night, by Zoe's bed, for one quick moment she thought he was preparing to unleash it. He would never hurt Zoe, would he?

She wants to ask Bob about it. At first she had forbidden

Bob from bringing Poe up in their conversations. Poe is the father of her children. He calls her his wife, which she tolerates to an extent. He even put his name on Zoe's birth certificate, which angered Bob. Bob called Poe weird and a nerd. Sometimes he called him dangerous, and that was *before* the beating.

Last night was one of those nights. She wanted it to be sweet. Poe touched her panties from behind. That's not *her* Poe! That's not Poe and all his quirks she finds so amusing. Calling black people *brown*. Calling Gerardo *Bryce*. Calling her his wife. That is the fun stuff. Something that young doctor had said that she dismissed comes back to her. The kids are alphabetized.

Zoe Yasmine. Xavier William. Victor Ulysses.

Dangerous.

The toilet paper, overcome with tears, has dissolved into a soggy clump. She goes into a bathroom so clean it sparkles. As she tears off a few sheets she breathes in the clean. Poe has used a new air freshener. It smells like apples.

Dangerous.

She sits on the toilet to clear her head. The Periwinkle Killer alphabetizes his victims.

Dangerous.

And that broken nose. An accident at work. Pizza work? Someone knocks on the door. At this hour? It must be Poe. He has a key. Why doesn't he use it? *Did I leave the chain on again?*

She leaves the bathroom. The knock comes again. She goes to the front door and peeps through the peep.

It's dark, but the person steps back, giving her a peephole view of a tall black woman in a denim cap. There are other people around her, in bulky body armor carrying assault weapons at the ready. The tall black woman holds up a badge to the peep. The hunter's wife opens the door. The assault weapons remain raised at the ready.

"What do you want?" says the hunter's wife. "Why are you here?"

"Why do *you* think we're here?" The tall woman grips the silver handle of the sidearm in her holster. She pushes her head inside for quick look around the room. She says, "Is he here?"

"No."

"You sure?" She is a black woman in black. Her shirt, jeans, and short lace-up boots with sensible heels are all black. Her sidearm is black with a platinum grip. She wears aviator sunglasses at night.

"I can't believe it. I won't believe it," the hunter's wife says.

"Believe what?" the woman in black says.

"Whatever it is you say he's done."

"We haven't said anything yet."

"Well, what are you saying? Why are you here? What do you think he's done?"

The black detective signals the officers in armor, and they push past her and the hunter's wife into the well-ordered living room. They pass through the apartment, leading with their guns. Watching them, the hunter's wife thinks with alarm, *They're going to wake the kids. Poe insists the kids get eight hours of sleep.*

"We're not saying he did it, but he's a person of interest. We just want to talk to him." The black detective steps inside the apartment. She reminds the hunter's wife of Bob, same confident bearing, same dark complexion, same sensible heels, but her thoughts are pulled away from these observations. She nervously watches the uniformed officers handle Poe's things. They might knock over some of his carefully arranged things. They are tracking up the floor with their dirty boots. Poe will be so angry . . .

Dangerous.

"Don't hurt him," the hunter's wife says. "We've got kids. I just had a baby."

The detective nods. "We'll try."

She takes no comfort in the black detective's words. These rough men in their body armor, the terrible weapons they have brought—she is not deceived. She knows what it means, for she is the hunter's wife.

The hunter's wife is wise beyond her years.

Heidi

March 2000

The address was in Coral Gables, in a four-story building near the campus of the University of Miami. The hunter had been to this building before but not to this apartment. Apartment 307. He knocked. The door opened.

"Poe!"

"Heidi."

She reached up to his broad shoulders, brought his face down for a face kiss. Another surprise—she kissed him on the mouth. The pizza nearly spilled from the warmer bag balanced on his left shoulder.

"Come in. Come in," she said.

He stood there in a daze, the warmer bag buzzing with warmth on his shoulder against his face. He hadn't seen her since he was a child. Her hair in glistening black ringlets fell across the left side of her face like it did back then. Her oval-shaped brown eyes used to fascinate him. They seem filled with honey, and when she smiled they disappeared into slits. Now, behind a pair of square-rimmed spectacles, they appeared larger, more intelligent, but she was no less beautiful.

"Come in. We'll share the pizza," she said.

"Munchie Luciano's has a rule strictly forbidding us to eat any of the pizzas we deliver."

She grabbed his hand. "Screw that," she said. "Come in. Come in."

Against his protests, she pulled him into a small apartment that had clean white walls but was untidy with books. To make room for him on the couch, she brushed aside a stack of books.

"Sit," she said.

He set the pizza box on an aluminum end table, the cheap kind sold in college bookstores, and sat.

She plunked down next to him. "Well, isn't this something?"

"Yes, it is something."

She wore yellow Tweety Bird shorts under a blue terry-cloth robe. The robe was short and loose-fitting. It was tied with a terry-cloth sash. There was no shirt beneath the robe that he could see, just the shorts. She smelled like the lilac soap his wife bathed with. When she moved, the robe shifted and her belly button was exposed. He averted his eyes.

"You proposed to me, remember?" she said. "You promised you'd marry me when you grew up."

They nodded their heads and laughed. He was seven back then. She was sixteen. When the shower suddenly shut off, the pipes in the ceiling of the small apartment groaned. They both looked up at the ceiling. They laughed again.

"Stephen," she said, pointing to where the shower sound had come from, but not explaining, not that it mattered. The hunter was already married. But who was Stephen? Didn't they shower together? The hunter always showered with his wife. That was the best part of taking a shower.

Between bites of pizza and swallows of canned soda, she asked questions about life, how has life been, how, how, how, and oh—

"I haven't seen you since before I left for college. You've grown up so handsome," she said.

He had grown to 6'2". His show-off arms and legs, which she had studied since opening the door, were a result of slavish devotion to the gym. He wore a fashionable mustache, which his wife had encouraged him to grow so as to draw attention away from his freckles and mismatched ears.

"Mom said that you got a girl . . ."

"Pregnant," he said.

"Boy or girl?"

"Boy."

"I was married, then divorced. I had to get away from him. He was a monster. Then I got with Stephen." She lowered her voice. Her animated face became sad. "He's not much better," she said. Then she brightened. "I'm working at the *Herald* now. I'm a reporter."

"I love your articles."

"Love?"

"Well, your articles—they're good." He bit into a slice of the hot pizza. "They are well written and unbiased," he said with a mouth full of hot pizza.

"Really?" she said, lifting a slice, touching it to her lips.

"Well, especially those on killers." He set the slice on a napkin on the aluminum end table and recited from memory the entire article she had written about Richard Rogers.

Before real estate investor Richard Rogers set his 5-bedroom Harbor Beach "bungalow" on fire, killing his wife and her sister, he swapped their heads. Suzanne Green-Rogers's head was set in place on her sister Tabitha Green's neck, and the sister's head on Mrs. Green-Rogers's neck . . .

—She was impressed.

"I have a good memory," he said.

"No. It's more than that," she said. "That is absolutely amazing."

"I have a good memory," he said again, reaching for the pizza. "I know the electron configuration of every element on the periodic table."

"What?"

"Chemistry."

"Chemistry. Right. I remember all that junk we had to learn. I barely passed the class. In college I majored in journalism. I minored in history." A noise came from the bathroom and she turned her head. It was the sound of water, running from a sink faucet this time. Stephen was brushing his teeth. A toilet flushed. She turned back to him. "Have you memorized any more articles?"

"Just yours."

"Really? How many?"

"Most of them. All of the ones about serial killers. Uh-oh. That didn't come out right," he said. He took a bite of pizza, swallowed. A childlike smile appeared on his face. "I'm just saying, you write about them so well."

"Well, I'm writing a book on them, and my dad—"

"Yeah," he said. "I remember my folks talking about it."

"They say he skipped town, but I have a feeling that's not what happened."

The toilet flushed again and Stephen, a tall, lanky, light-haired man with a handsome all-American face, walked out. He wore a terry-cloth robe of the same color as Heidi's. Beneath the robe he wore the yellow Tweety Bird shorts.

Introductions were made all around. Stephen grabbed two slices, and sat across from them in an aluminum folding chair, the kind sold at college bookstores. When Stephen moved, his robe shifted and his belly button was exposed. The hunter only had eyes for Heidi.

Stephen had a reporter's instincts. He regarded the hunter with suspicion. The hunter had not made his first kill yet, so it couldn't be about that. Maybe Stephen was simply jealous. Husbands are like that. You come out of the shower and your wife is eating pizza with the pizza man. Jealousy like that can kill. Stephen had no need to be jealous. Heidi and the hunter were just childhood friends. The babysitter and the babysat. Just old friends who couldn't take their eyes off each other. Just friends who looked at each other as though they shared a secret.

Run!

From a pay phone, the hunter calls his wife.

"What happened to Bob is not enough."

"Poe . . ."

"It's not enough."

"Poe . . . I know he was a killer, but I . . . still feel something for him . . . His head was smashed. He was hit so hard his eyes popped out." She sucks back tears. "Nobody deserves to die that way."

"Bob did."

"No, Poe. He didn't. He's dead. Can't you forgive?"

"I can't."

"I love you."

"No you don't."

"I do."

"How can you say you do?" He furiously wipes tears from his face. "You humiliated me. You said you wanted us both. How do you think that made me feel?"

"I shouldn't have said that. I shouldn't have been with him. I'm horrible. I'm trash," the hunter's wife says. "But I love you." There is a sound behind her, like something metallic falling, hitting the ground. Is the call being traced?

"Don't come home, Poe!" the hunter's wife says. "Run!" she says.

Someone takes the phone from her. A smoky voice awakens the hairs on his skin.

"Periwinkle," the brown detective says.

Sad face.

5

"Poe Edgar Jackson, be silent and listen," the brown detective says. "We know about Bob. It was all about Bob. You beat him up that day. You wanted to get him for sleeping with your girlfriend."

"My wife."

"What?"

"My wife."

"I thought she said she was your . . . Okay. We went to the pizza restaurant tonight to arrest you. The phone was torn out of the wall. I know you're angry. Make it easy on yourself. Turn yourself in. You found out Montgomery was the Snatcher. You got him for us. You rescued Jermaine. He loves you, by the way. He says you're his hero. A jury might find that compelling. They may not give you the death penalty."

"Now," the hunter says, "*you* be silent and listen."

6

In his farcical voice he says, "Take notes. Fill out forms. Clean up. That's all you do. Sixteen years he was banging white women."

"Poe Edgar Jackson, turn yourself—"

"Didn't you see the resemblance in the children? Shame on you, you of all people, my dear brown detective—do all brown children look the same to you?"

"Make it easy on yourself," the brown detective says. "If you don't surrender, we will come after you now that we know who you are—"

"Mary!" the hunter shouts, hoping she can hear his voice. "I love you!"

"It's not too late for you," says the brown detective.

"Tell the kids I love them, Mary!"

"You have a chance if you give yourself up."

"Mary, I forgive you!"

"Give yourself up. They don't execute insane people," the brown detective says.

The hunter chuckles slyly. "They don't execute insane people?" He returns to his farcical voice. "Tehehe. Oh, it's too late for me. I killed one of your own tonight, Detective."

"We're coming to get you, Periwinkle!" the brown detective says. "You're gonna get it!"

Smiley face.

Motel La Image

He steals the license tag from a Cadillac in a Burger King parking lot. He screws it in place on the old Buick. He drives west-northwest on Okeechobee Road into South Hialeah. He slips two sticks of peppermint gum in his mouth. Not thick enough. When it becomes powder, he slips in a third.

He checks into the one-star motel—La Image.

The desk clerk, chewing on the stub of an unlit cigar, does not look up. He wears a grimy white T-shirt and is balanced on a high stool behind a filthy bulletproof glass barrier. He is a fat man in need of a shave. He is obese. He asks no questions as the hunter swings twenty dollars in singles to him on a turret in the bulletproof glass. When the turret swings back, there's a key on it: room 17.

A single, dim bulb lights the hallway where three women lean against the wall smoking cigarettes—prostitutes most likely. Only one of their cigarettes is really a cigarette. They wear blond wigs and thick makeup. They give the hunter a bored glance, then watch with amusement as he hauls his garbage bag of equipment past them and into room 17.

The floor is covered in hair and dirt. There are brown stains on the wall and yellow stains on the sheets. He has brought soap, Lysol, bleach, a hand broom, and sponges. He scrapes and wipes and sprays and sweeps until the room is livable. It smells nice. Lemony fresh. He has brought his own sheets.

He calls his favorite journalist.

"I'm away from my desk right now. Please leave a message at the sound of the tone."

"When I needed your comfort, you didn't pick up. The problems in my marriage persisted until . . . But it's not about my woes. It's about your dad. I know where he is. Here's the number where you can reach me . . ."

The hunter stretches out on the clean sheets with the dead man's head balanced on his stomach. The Dolphins cap sits at a jaunty angle on the thick head. The hunter lifts it off the head and fondles it until he falls asleep.

The Emporium on West Andrews Avenue

In the morning, Dada awakes him: *Leave now.*

He gets up. He collects his things. He steals a license tag from a Dodge Caravan in the parking lot and screws it on the old Buick. All day he drives around the city. When the sun sets he drives north to Broward. He finds a better one-star motel.

The Emporium on Andrews has a shower and a mini kitchen in each room. The Emporium on Andrews also advertises a pool.

When he pulls up to the fleabag motel, he finds the pool has been drained and is being used for containment of the motel's broken bathroom sinks, a stack of three doorless refrigerators, and a mound of plumbing ducts and piping.

Though the condition of the pool is a disappointment, the interior of the Emporium on West Andrews is an upgrade from La Image. The floors in the lobby have been swept and the freshly painted terra-cotta walls smell like pine needles as the paint is still drying. In the dim hallway, the prostitutes sporting blond wigs and smoking cigarettes are clean. Behind the bulletproof glass, the clerk is younger and speaks.

"Room?"

"One night."

The clerk nods, and the exchange of twenty dollars for a key is made.

Room 12.

The hunter asks, "Is room 17 available?"

"No."

"There is no way I can have 17?"

"No," the clerk says. "Enjoy."

Seventeen has always been lucky for him. He considers going to another motel, but he can't. This is all he can afford on a night with no tips. He noisily drags his garbage bag of tools down the hallway to his room. He opens the door to room 12 and shakes his head.

"Don't they ever clean?" the hunter says.

He unpacks his soap, Lysol, bleach, hand broom, and sponges. He scrapes and wipes and sweeps and shines. He unfolds his sheets and spreads them over the bed smoothly, each tail fit to its corner tight enough to please a drill sergeant. Once again, cleaning a room has calmed him. Standing by the freshly made bed, a fluffed pillow in his hands, he is overcome by a bleak realization and runs into the bathroom and vomits in the sink. His once-ordered world is a shambles. He leans over the sink again, but nothing comes up. He wipes his mouth with a hand towel he has brought. He goes back out to the bedroom for a sponge, scrubber brush, and baking soda to clean the sink a second time. As he cleans, words he's never considered pass through his lips.

"Maybe I could've killed Bob without having to kill the others."

Then he remembers Eduardo's wife-beating, David's adultery, Carl's predations on the innocent, Arne the bad cop, and he is disgusted all over again.

"They got what they deserved."

The old Buick is parked outside in the motel's parking lot. He had fled in it after dumping the pizza van at his mother's. He peeps out the window at it and his mind runs on his favorite journalist.

"She knew the old Buick when it was new," he says to himself. How could you not fall for someone you connect with on that level? He didn't touch her even after her second husband moved out, though he had always liked her.

How could a boy not have a crush on his old babysitter?

He didn't touch her, though they grew closer. He remained faithful to his marriage vows. But being a seventeen-year-old father, losing Andrea—he was hurt, angry, and weak, and Heidi listened. She was hurt, angry, and weak also, having a husband who was an unrepentant libertine.

And so it happened. A little boy's fantasy became a reality. He got to kiss his babysitter.

—She listened. She understood.

She helped him get over the pain of losing Bryce. She knew what losing someone you love was like, having lost her father, who had disappeared without a trace. She understood Poe's pain when he spoke about Bryce.

"That night in the tree house, he was trying to tell me he was in trouble, but he was always so cool, had everything under control, and I was so caught up in my stuff I couldn't hear he was crying out for help. Then he came to my house looking for me. I wasn't there for him. He hung himself in my backyard."

"You were the best friend you could've been," she said.

"He left the suicide note for me. It was not even a suicide note. It was advice on love. *Stay away from Mary. Fight for Andrea. Be with the one you love. True love is worth it.* I didn't get the chance to tell him how things had changed. How I had fallen in love with Mary. How we cuddled. What Mary and I had was true love. But see, that's not the point. His father kicked him out, he had nowhere to sleep, but even before he put that rope around his neck, he was concerned with me and my problems—my petty high school drama. I should've been there for him."

"The contents of the note are not as important as the fact that he left it for *you*, not his parents," she told him. "He was concerned with you right to the very end. This tells me that he loved you. The note was not about dying, but about living. As long as you live, he survives. He'll always be there in your heart."

—And she helped him see that he had to fight for his marriage. When her parents divorced, it hurt so much. She told him that he had to be so good to his wife that she would forget Bob.

"If that doesn't work," she said, "then divorce is the only other option. When my parents divorced it hurt us kids, but it helped too. We didn't have to see them fight all the time."

"I love my wife."

"Do you?"

"Yes. She's pregnant, it may be his, but I love her."

"You're not being realistic," she said.

"I *am* being realistic," he said.

"You know what? I don't think I'm helping the situation," she said. "I don't think I'm helping it at all."

They parted, but as friends, after dating for a year. He would miss the talks, the just being there. He would miss the cuddling.

—*"I'm away from my desk right now. Please leave a message at the sound of the tone."*

"I wanted to talk, but you're away from your desk. You didn't call me last night at the Motel La Image. I'm at a new motel. I can't tell you where. If you can spare a few minutes to talk, call me back at this new number. They're after me and I don't know how long I have. They could break down the door any minute—"

She picks up in the middle of his explanation. "Where's my father? Did he abandon us?"

"He did not abandon you."

"I knew it," she says. "Is he alive?"

"No."

"Okay," she says. "I figured that," she says. "Tell me what happened. I'm sure your dad told you. They were best friends."

"You're writing that book on serial killers. You're a writer of exceptional talent—"

"My father, Poe. What about my father?" There is movement behind her. Is her estranged husband back in bed with her? For a moment he's jealous. He remembers the feel of her in his arms. "Just tell me," she says. There is a pause and when she resumes speaking, she is a reporter again. "Why're you calling so late?"

Another pause.

"Why're you calling from a motel? Who's after you?" she says.

"My dad would've loved the name you guys have given him. The Vitruvian Man."

"I don't understand."

"The Vitruvian Man killed your dad," Poe says.

She still doesn't understand.

"My dad was the Vitruvian Man."

A sharp gasp comes from her side of the phone, followed by the sound of crying.

Now she understands.

—"I wanted to tell you so many times."

"Your father killed my dad, and you knew?"

"You helped me with Bryce. You helped me save my marriage."

"All this time you knew and you didn't tell me?" she says. Then she lowers her voice. There is definitely someone in bed with her. She whispers, "You fucked me, Poe. Your dad killed my dad, you knew, and we fucked. What kind of monster are you?"

"I am Periwinkle," he says, and there comes another sharp gasp from her side of the phone. "Heidi?"

—"Heidi?"

"I want the exclusive," she says through sobs. "Don't let them get you before you've told me everything."

"I'd rather talk about old times."

"The murders, Poe. The murders."

"Okay," he says.

—"Open the door to a pizza man and you present a snapshot of your life. Order routinely and it's like the slideshows they showed us in elementary school. Not quite a movie, not quite a book, but a series of snapshots that tell the story of you. Eduardo, for example, ordered pizza three times before I chose him. His wife opened the door the first time. She was six months pregnant, and she had a black eye. The second time I delivered, her arm was in a sling. The third time, Eduardo came to the door. I saw her behind him, preparing the table, hobbled on crutches, one leg in a cast. She was no longer pregnant. What happened to the baby? Did she lose the baby when she tripped and fell by accident, as she told the nurses in the emergency room? Or did she lose it when he threw her down a flight of stairs? I had the snapshots. I knew the truth. Eduardo was my first victim."

He pauses for effect.

"The second victim, David, was a whoremonger, but that's not even the point. People are free to cheat. I mean, *we* cheated."

"*You* cheated," she says. "I had already divorced Stephen."

"Yes, but you knew I was married."

"Mary is your girlfriend."

"We live together. She is the mother of my children. It's still infidelity."

"On your part."

"Okay. Let's agree to disagree," he says. "I followed David's mistress. She and her husband fought all the time about *her* infidelity. He was a drunk. I felt like killing him too, but that would've left the kids orphaned. Now Carl, the pedophile, was more straightforward. He was easy to stalk. The world is better without him. Bob slept with my wife. You know that already. Arne, the final rat, made the news for shooting a child. You wrote about it. I could recite your article if you'd like."

"No thank you," she says.

"Have it your way then."

"You think you're a hero, don't you?"

"Yes."

"You're not a hero. You're a murderer. If I'm figuring this right, you were stalking Eduardo while we were dating—before you knew Mary was with Bob."

"I was after Eduardo because he was a wife beater. Beat her so bad she lost a child. I hadn't planned to kill him, just wanted to talk to him. Give him a good beating like he did her. Let him see how it feels. But then my wife told me about Bob. That 'E' was a coincidence, and they'd better be glad I started with it or there'd be twenty-six dead rats."

"But this is crazy."

"They deserved to die."

"No they didn't."

"You sound like my wife."

"Your girlfriend."

"Once again, we agree to disagree." He adjusts his body so that the thick head is balanced on his chest. "There is a picture of Bryce and me in Disney caps on the nightstand on my side of the bed. I hid Dada's notes in the frame." He pinches Thick Face's nose playfully. "My notes are in another frame, one with a picture of a family on a boat—professional models. The frame is gold. It's on a high shelf in the children's room. It's next to a hideous lamp. You can't miss it," he says. "And that's it."

"That's it?"

"That's it," he says.

"Poe?"

"Heidi?"

"Give yourself up."

"Tehehe."

Clean Sheets for Foul

At 4:47 a.m., Dada wakes him from a dream.

In the dream he had no hands.

Leave now.

The hunter gets up. He returns Thick Face's head and other things to the plastic garbage bag to dump them at the site he will use on the way out of Florida—but to where?

Nebraska, Dada says.

"In Nebraska, I'll find Cassidy and disappear him."

Do it, but leave now, Dada says. *Hurry.*

In the lobby of the Emporium there is a wall of colorful discount pamphlets, folded maps, and glossy tourist guides. He takes a map, and back in his room he sits on the bed and unfolds it. He checks for the most traveled routes to Altoona so that he can avoid them. In Altoona there are famous hot springs. Alexander Springs. He has heard the ground near the hot springs is rich. The thick head will disappear there. The bloody T-shirt and gun will be buried there too. The Dolphins cap, however, is crying out from the bag not to be disappeared. He lifts it out and brings it to his nose. Dandruff, a few thin strands of graying hair, microscopic scrapings of skin, a crust of dried blood on the brim. He cannot keep the cap. The smell would leave him in a permanent state of arousal. He would need a new wife. A wave of regret washes over him.

Ah, Mary.

Despite all she has done, he loves his wife. She stood by

him in sickness and in health. She gave him three children and Zoe, little brown Zoe, Zoe Montgomery, whom he loves as much as the others.

Ah, Mary.

He cheated first.

She didn't know about Heidi. She didn't know what was broken in the marriage, but she felt the damage and found comfort in the filthy sheets of Bob—Bob, a man she wouldn't cuddle with afterward; Bob, who was not as good in bed as the hunter.

They are separate and apart on most things, but on this they agree: cuddling after sex means love.

"She never stopped cuddling with me," he says to the faded wallpaper of the run-down motel room. "The marriage is only damaged. It can still be repaired. I love her—"

There is a clicking sound, and he turns his ear to the door.

Poe

They are here.

The scratching of weapons against denim. The sound of boots crunching dirt on the filthy floor. The collective breathing of huddled, crouching men. Theirs is a noisy silence, these small, innocuous sounds—they bang a cacophony for someone who has been expecting them for four years.

The room has a second door, a side door that communicates with another room. He hears them in that room too.

He takes the gun out of Thick Face's bag and shoves the barrel in his mouth.

Periwinkle

Dada says, *Gird up your loins. Take it like a man.*

He removes Thick Face's gun from his mouth and returns it to the bag. Hatchet and rapier shall be his final arms. He slips a stick of peppermint gum in his mouth and crouches, waiting for them.

He laughs loudly, and the people hiding on the other side of the door abandon their silence.

Someone announces, "Poe Edgar Jackson, come out with your hands up!"

"Make me."

"This is your last warning!"

"Bring it!"

Both doors, front and side, burst open.

The hunter is a big man and strong. He launches himself against the first hard plastic shield that comes through the door, knocking the man holding it to the ground, pushing back the throng, amazingly pushing them off balance, knocking them over like dominoes. He surges over the fallen man, mounts his chest, swinging. The rapier is mostly useless, but he gets one with the hatchet—lops the hand clean off at the wrist, and it flies.

He watches it fly.

SWAT pushes him back with their shields. He is shoved against the bed, but does not topple over. He stands tall, a toothy grin on his face. They begin firing.

His chest is hit with a hailstorm of bullets. Chunks of his shoulder are scooped out. One bullet lodges in his throat.

His legs give way and he falls back on the neatly made bed, his arms spread wide like Christ on the cross. His face is still intact. His eyes are open. He is smiling. What does he see?

Now the ones from the side door who had restrained from firing so as not to shoot their comrades coming through the front door commence firing. Theirs are mostly head shots. The hunter's smile is torn away along with his mouth as his head disintegrates.

The hunter is a dead man, but the police keep firing, punching holes in everything in the room, just in case.

One of them cries out, "My hand, my hand, my hand! Oh God, my hand!"

The police keep firing until small red flames sprout like flowers from the mattress. Smoke and the smell of gunpowder choke the air.

The same man cries, "My hand! Oh God, my hand!"

They keep firing. The sound of rapid-fire explosions is deafening.

WHERE THE BONES ARE BURIED

Funeral Service

The law enforcement community grieved yesterday as one of its own, Officer Arne Duncan, a twenty-year veteran of the Miami-Dade Police Department, was laid to rest at the historic Caballero Rivero Wood-lawn Memorial Gardens on Coral Way.

Duncan is the sixth law enforcement officer to be killed in the state of Florida this year and the fifth confirmed victim of the serial killer known as Periwinkle.

Many remember when Arne Duncan made the news for his high-profile case of alleged police brutality against a Black teen in a stolen car.

Duncan, who believed 13-year-old Tyrese McNair was reaching for a gun when his hand ducked below the window to hide a marijuana joint he had been smoking, could not see clearly because it was night and the windows were tinted. He fired twice into the stolen car.

Duncan also saved the wounded McNair's life by providing emergency medical treatment to him while enduring angry epithets being hurled at him by the agitated mob that had gathered.

"Only a life lived in service to others is worth living," a quote from Albert Einstein, will be engraved on Duncan's headstone.

—Heidi Renoir-Smith, *Miami Herald*

Absent Husbands

Periwinkle. The Vitruvian Man.

For me, it's a cruel irony. I'm collecting material for a book on serial killers, and I knew two of them as a child.

Poe Edgar Jackson and I share the same birthday. He was born the day I turned nine. June 25, 1982. My father disappeared a month later.

Our families were close. We lived a few houses away from each other in Palmetto Grove. We worshipped at the same Presbyterian church. Our fathers, who had known each other since childhood, were best friends.

As a teenager, I babysat Poe so that I could buy things like designer jeans, CDs, and cigarettes when I got into that. When he grew up and I came back to town, he delivered pizza to my apartment a few times. He was always kind to his old babysitter, refusing to take a tip unless I insisted. My mother told me that he had done well in school, but had gotten his girlfriend pregnant.

Gone was the odd boy I had babysat. He was handsome now, and fit. I remembered feeling sad for him because none of the other children would play with him. I remembered his disturbing laugh.

I remembered the day I found him peeling the dead rat. I quickly took the knife away and had him throw the rat in the dumpster out back. I was chilled by the sight of it. And what if he had cut himself? I would get in trouble. And oh, how gross. A child skinning a rat.

His mother became angry when I told her. His father proved to be more understanding. Father and son huddled close and spoke in low tones. Then his father told us he would take the knife and put it somewhere safe. This was the same knife, a small replica of a fifteenth-century rapier, that his father, we now know, had used in many of his own killings.

Poe's father, Edgar L. Jackson, was himself a serial murderer. The victims of Edgar L. Jackson, who is now being called the Vitruvian Man because of the mathematical precision with which he displayed the body parts of his victims, number more than two dozen. The elder Jackson kept meticulous notes. He was obsessive about cleanliness. He was fanatical about order and routine. These are traits he passed on to his son.

My mother remained friends with Poe's mother after his father went to prison. Absent husbands—they had that in common.

My father went first, disappeared off the map.

Jackson's went second, incarcerated for murder.

We suspected foul play when my father went missing. The police suspected the fairly common practice of a divorced man unable to meet his financial obligations to his children and ex-wife. Skip town. Leave no forwarding address.

I did not believe this about my father, whom I remembered as a kind, protective, loving parent. He was playful and indulgent. Though he lived in a *cramped and messy trailer, we loved our time over there. He had no temper that I ever witnessed. He spoiled us. He taught us to play pool. He taught us to swim in a pool. My father would not abandon us, and his trailer—where was the familiar and pleasant messiness? My father, who could not care less about neatness, had left his trailer perfectly clean. No, this was not my daddy. Something had happened to him.*

But I was nine when he disappeared, just a kid. What did I know? I was told to keep my opinions about my father to myself.

Charlemagne Renoir. Poe told us where to find his dad's notes. Those notes told us where to find my father.

He was planted in a cow pasture on the east side of I-75 near an abandoned playground. The bottoms of his shoes were visible under a thin layer of cement. My mother recognized the favorite shoes of her first husband and let out a cry that would startle the quick and wake the dead.

They used heavy machinery to break the cement. Then, with careful, practiced hands, they exhumed what was left of him from his resting place. My brother Bobby, the youngest of us, fainted. My sister Claire, the investment banker, the most sober and level-headed of us, had to be hospitalized. For a week my eyes burned from crying.

But I was right all along. My father had not abandoned us. He was murdered by his best friend, Edgar L. Jackson.

I am happy for Jermaine Milkovich, the 10-year-old Snatcher victim we had all been praying for until he was rescued by Periwinkle earlier this month.

Little Jermaine had met two monsters and survived.
Some of us didn't.
  Some of us never will.

—Heidi Renoir-Smith, op-ed, *Miami Herald*

I had to know

Knowledge can be painful.

When Poe called from the motel where he had taken refuge, the casual way he spoke about my father's murder angered me. I needed him to be caught and punished for his crimes.

*After we hung up, I dialed *69 and a rough voice answered: "Emporium Motel. Whaddaya want?"*

Rude.

I hung up. Poe was at the Emporium Motel. That's all I needed to know. And now I knew. The next number I dialed was the police. Now they knew.

One could argue that I was responsiblve for Poe's death. Sometimes knowing hurts.

Sometimes knowing hurts.

I do not think I have the courage to put this next part in my book. In fact, I won't. I do not think Poe was aware. I hope he wasn't.

One night when I ordered pizza, Poe delivered it and a birthday card. I was caught off guard by the birthday card. I had been working so hard on an assignment at the time that I had worked straight through my birthday. Our birthday. I found a candle and lit it. We sang happy birthday to ourselves, blew out the candle, and shared the pizza. We looked into each other's eyes. The next thing we knew, he had delivered more than a pizza, and I had given more than a tip.

We dated 12 months and 12 days. He said it was wrong. He said he loved his girlfriend. I was falling for him, to be honest. Then he told me she was pregnant again. That was the deal-breaker. I became angry. So it ended. On the rebound, I went back to my estranged husband until I realized I didn't love him. I have to be honest. I missed the sex with Poe. He loves like a man on fire.

In her grief, Poe's mother confessed that she and my father had been lovers. This affair is probably why the Vitruvian Man would murder my father, his best friend since childhood.

It was a simple question. My siblings refused to ask it, but I did. I had to know.

For a small funeral, it was large.

About two dozen other reporters showed up, along with a crowd of onlookers and protesters carrying signs and placards.

Monster. Murderer. Burn in Hell.

A cordon of uniformed officers stood between the protesters and the seven people gathered around his coffin at the hole: the officiating minister in a priestly white collar and black suit, two adult women in black veils, and three small children. The seventh person was an infant in its mother's arms.

I recognized them as his mother, Barbara-Jean, his girlfriend, Mary Fisk, and his children: Poe Edgar Jackson Jr., Zoe, Xavier, and the infant Victor. The little girl Zoe, his mixed-race stepdaughter who was fathered by the infamous child murderer Robert Montgomery, clung to her mother's hand.

For a large funeral, it was small.

No other family members came.

I pushed my way through the throng of reporters in an attempt to stand with the family. A police officer put up his hand, blocking me.

"You're a reporter," he said, no doubt recognizing me as the Herald's top crime reporter.

"I am, but I'm not on the job. I babysat him as a child. Ask his mother."

The chanting began: "Murderer! Murderer! Murderer!"

The officer went to Poe's mother and said something to her. She didn't even look up, but when he came back he said a gruff "Okay," and I was allowed to pass.

I went to his mother, a plump, round-faced woman with big eyes. Her midnight-black hair seemed to have gone gray over the week since the fight with my mother. I don't know why she confessed to the affair after all of these years, and I don't know why my mother got so angry over it. If anyone should've been angry, it was me and my siblings. We had lost our father. My mother had divorced him long before he had disappeared, and had remarried twice. I put my hand on Poe's mother's back. Crying, she leaned into me.

The chanting continued: "Murderer! Murderer! Burn in hell!"

From the mother's veil came a waterlogged voice: "You came here to ask the question."

"Is he?"

"The answer is no."

I had attended the funeral, thinking that if I got close enough, I could steal a strand of hair from the head of one of his children. I would give the strand along with a strand of my own to my friend who runs the clinic that tests DNA for paternity cases. I needed to know if the child and I share the same DNA.

His grieving mother said, "No. Poe is not his son."

I had interviewed enough liars to know better than to believe someone with her back against the wall.

The chanting grew unbearable: "Murderer! Murderer! Burn in hell!"

My head throbbed with a different refrain: Mama's baby. Papa's maybe. She's lying.

Before the funeral ended, I made my way over to Poe's girlfriend and embraced her and then the children, and I plucked a hair from Jr.'s head.

After debating with myself for a month, I gave Poe Edgar Jr.'s hair and one of my own to the friend who runs the paternity clinic. A week later the report came back in a manila envelope.

I left it sealed for a month.

Then I broke the seal, though I left it unsealed for another month without taking out the letter.

I didn't want to know the truth. I told myself that I could live just fine without knowing that the Periwinkle Killer shares my blood. I told myself that for someone writing a book on serial killers, a final irony of that sort would be too hard to bear. But a reporter who doesn't want to know the truth—what kind of reporter is that?

I read the results a minute ago. I wish I hadn't read them. Poe Edgar Jackson is my brother.

—From the notes of Heidi Renoir-Smith

Hurricane Season

Poe was correct.

The 2004 Florida hurricane season was the worst in the past hundred years. Four major storms came ashore in Florida. The storms caused more than thirty-eight billion dollars in damage and were responsible for eighty-seven deaths, thirty-one of them directly.

The Baby

In three years, Mary Eugenia Fisk marries again.

The babies when they are born are twins. She names the girl Judy after her favorite sister.

She names the boy Thomas as requested by her first husband Poe, whom she still loves.

Miami Serial Killers, 1965-2007
by Heidi Renoir-Smith

Chapter 1: **The Periwinkle Killer,** *Poe Edgar Jackson, the Pizza Man. Five murders confirmed—Jackson was killed by gunfire in a battle with police.*

Chapter 2: **Andrew "Andre" Cunanan.** *Killer of fashion icon Gianni Versace; killed as many as five—Cunanan committed suicide by gunshot.*

Chapter 3: **The Tamiami Strangler,** *Milton Edwin Pyle, the Handsome Hitchhiker. Killed as many as six—Pyle was executed in Florida's electric chair.*

Chapter 4: **The Snatcher,** *Robert Franklin "Bob" Montgomery, Flowers for the Dead. Killed as many as seven— Montgomery was murdered by the Periwinkle Killer.*

Chapter 5: **Monster,** *Aileen Wournos, the Killer Prostitute. Killed as many as seven—Wournos was executed in Florida's electric chair.*

Chapter 6: **The Handyman,** *Richard Rogers, the Millionaire Who Was Good with Tools. Eight murders confirmed, life sentence—Rogers died of natural causes after fifteen years in a Florida prison.*

Chapter 7: **The Medicine Woman,** *Mary Beth Standing Rain,* *the Killer Nurse. Killed as many as seventeen by poisoning, life sentence—Standing Rain died of natural causes after twenty-five years in a Florida prison.*

*Chapter 8: **The Vitruvian Man**, Edgar L. Jackson, Mathematical Precision. Killed as many as twenty-seven—Jackson was murdered in a Florida prison.*

Acknowledgments

For their support and advice, I would like to acknowledge the following: Benjamin Brown; Kevin Eady; Jason Murray; Nidley Charles; my talented family, the sibs and kids Allen, and especially Sherwin, who read five drafts of the novel; Quinn Allen aka "Qaaman" the top DragonaballZ YouTuber in the US, who read the book and among other things advised which words would get me canceled if I didn't remove them; my tireless agent Eleanor Jackson; my editor at Akashic Aaron Petrovich, who understood the novel and made it better; and Johnny Temple, who once again has championed this artist and is giving voice to his words.

Thank you all.